MIDWESTERN GOTHIC

SPRING 2015
ISSUE 17

Midwestern Gothic Issue 17 (Spring 2015)

To learn more about us and our mission, or for more information on our submissions policy, please visit our website or email us at MWGothic@gmail.com.

Subscriptions: 1 year (4 issues) - $40 (print) / $10 (digital)

www.midwestgothic.com

ISSN: 2159-8827
ISBN: 9780988201378

Cover photo copyright © David J. Thompson

MIDWESTERN
GOTHIC

FICTION EDITORS
Jeff Pfaller
Robert James Russell

POETRY EDITOR
Christina Olson

COPY EDITORS
J. Joseph Kane
Jessica Dewberry
Mackenzie Meter
C.J. Opperthauser

EDITORIAL ASSISTANT
Lauren Crawford

INTERNS
Cammie Finch
Jamie Monville
Kelly Nhan

READERS
Jon Michael Darga
Graham Dethmers
Stephanie Mezzanatto

COVER IMAGE
David J. Thompson

BOOK DESIGN
Jeff Pfaller

CONTENTS

PSYCHIATRIST
COREY MERTES

She wakes up, but before her eyes are open her body knows that she is alone. The odor of fried pig fat confirms that Rob is up before her, making breakfast. It's an awful stench. With her eyes still closed she runs through the mental exercises she uses to banish negative thoughts. Gradually, her brow unfurls and she can open her eyes and embrace the morning. *It's only bacon.* The sunlight, so beautiful, slants in through the open blinds. Her smile reflects warmth as she recalls—and how could she forget!—that she is Mrs. Allie Martin. She vows to greet her husband of three months with the energy and optimism he deserves.

"Perfect timing," he says as they kiss. "I was just coming to wake you." He slides two poached eggs onto a plate alongside the bacon and toast he's prepared and gives her shoulder a squeeze. She grimaces, because he's disturbed a tender area he bruised the night before while they were making love—too brusquely, she thought at the time, but didn't want to ruin the moment, and likewise now doesn't let him see her wince.

"Aren't you eating?"

"Mm," he takes a quick bite of toast. "I'm meeting Ben. I'm late already."

The scattered papers on the table indicate he's been working since early morning. He gathers them along with the book he takes everywhere, *Success in 10 Simple Rules.* Ben is Ben Carlson, founder of Ben Carlson Studios—their benefactor, as Rob likes to joke. Of the two BCS ballroom dance clubs in town, Ben operates the original and franchises the other to Rob, who, like the dozen other franchisees around the country, pays Ben a percentage for use of the BCS teaching system and name. Lately Rob has been trying to work out an arrangement with Ben that will grant him independence while allowing him to continue participating in the BCS showcases convened biannually, where members and instructors from all the clubs gather to perform routines on a grand stage. It's a big selling point. The show is followed by a formal ball. Allie is currently at work on two numbers, including a cha-cha with her newest Bronze student for a performance next Sunday at the first event hosted locally in years.

"How's that going?" she asks.

He kisses the top of her head. "Don't you worry," he says. "You haven't touched your breakfast."

She punctures one of the eggs with a fork. "Hon. Sweetie, you know I'm not eating bacon or eggs on this new diet. I'll have some melon when you're gone."

"Don't be silly, you'll need all your strength today. What time is Joe?"

She knows he knows when her lesson with Joe Stevens is, it's been marked in red on his office calendar for a week. They're trying him for the full Bronze program today—fourteen thousand dollars. "Two o'clock," she says, nibbling a piece of toast.

"Nobody needs the Bronze like Joe does. Overweight. Balding. Insecure."

"He understands that."

"He has to feel it," Rob says, squeezing her shoulders again. This is a refrain she's heard a thousand times since she began teaching there after a year as his student. She winces again, assures him that Joe feels the magic, and scoops a whole egg into her mouth as if to confirm it.

"That's my girl," he says. "I know he does."

After he leaves, Allie, having violated her diet, sees no reason not to finish her plate; then she unwraps the rest of the bacon and fries it along with four more eggs. As it all sizzles, she reviews the benefits to Joe Stevens of a two-year membership—longer individual sessions, group lessons every week, unlimited parties—before catching herself, remembering that these are not benefits but features. She begins again: gracefulness; confidence in social settings; improved self-esteem. She must present these to Joe in a way that makes him feel like she felt when she was a student. Of course, she learned from the very best. "Dancing should be like great sex!" Rob rhapsodized during their first tango lesson. Today, with Joe, she is determined to channel that same irresistible vitality.

She butters two slices of toast, consumes them with the bacon and eggs, and follows it all with yogurt and a bowl of ice cream. Joe understands. Correction: Joe feels it. He has a good teacher, she thinks, remembering Rule 8: Compliment yourself daily. Then she smiles to herself too because, as Rob says, it's impossible to be negative when you're smiling—a variation of Rule 5.

Upstairs, she hangs up clothes Rob has left on the floor. Kelly wishes she were in my shoes, Allie tells herself. She would never admit it, but I know it's true, everybody says so. Even now she clings to some impossible fantasy, even though she's with Sean. I can tell when Rob works with her. What's more, Sean isn't going to marry her. I don't know why she can't see that.

A book of matches falls from Rob's pants to the floor. He's been on the patch for weeks but still sneaks an occasional cigarette, she can tell from the odor in his hair. She hopes it isn't more than a few because he really wants to quit, believing it hurts the studio's image. She notices they're from Mama Stuffiti's. Good, she thinks. They're old. They haven't been to Mama's in five months, since the night they agreed to marry. Rob must have kept them for sentimental reasons, the dear. Only a few matches are missing. Good again, he's not sneaking too many.

She folds his pants on the way to the bathroom where she bends over the toilet and, for the first time since before her miscarriage three weeks prior to the wedding, sticks a finger down her throat, causing her to vomit. At the sink, she wipes her mouth with the back of her hand, brushes her teeth and flosses. As she takes a dozen vitamins three at a time, she thinks, I hope Rob doesn't break with Ben the way Ben broke with Arthur Murray's—what a nasty lawsuit everyone says that was! Worrying that he'd better be careful, that Ben Carlson can be vicious when money is at stake, she removes the matches again from Rob's pocket and fingers them unconsciously, before dropping them in the wastebasket and swallowing the acid residue at the back of her throat.

*   *   *

Ben is still at the studio when she arrives, talking to Rob at the reception desk. He greets her with a hug and then holds her away at arms' length.

"Look at you," he says. "That blonde hair. Still the prettiest girl in the business. Rob, how did you corral the prettiest girl in the business?"

"She's trying Joe Stevens for Bronze today."

Allie can see her reflection distorted in Ben's large, nearly round tinted glasses. "Well, I'm sure she'll do just fine," he says, and she thinks she can see his thirsty eyes enlarge behind the brown lenses as he squeezes her hands. "How could he resist?" he adds, revealing that impish smile he's earned after thirty years of financial triumphs.

He and Rob finish talking privately as Allie changes into her dance shoes. She has a lesson with the Watsons before Joe is due in. A sweet couple, Allie's first full Bronze sale more than a year ago. Loretta was hooked from the beginning, since her introduction at their first party to some of the more advanced couples and club ambassadors. Bill Watson, permanently ungraceful, was less inspired but will do anything for his wife. They have time and money in their retirement and bought the whole package without the hard sell from Rob. He was so proud of her that day, the day she first knew she was in love.

When they arrive, Allie hugs them and leads them onto the floor. By now she can sleepwalk through their lessons, and her mind wanders to the other instructors. Travis is there with one of his lonely old ladies. Their sessions consist of him dragging them around the room as he complains about former boyfriends and they go on about their deteriorating health. Kelly is there also, she knows it first by the laugh. Allie contends that Kelly's staccato laughter is phony, but Rob disagrees. He is on the floor too, with Mrs. Shapiro, running through the quick step he's choreographed for their upcoming performance. His lessons are all smiles and grace and pinpoint instruction. The king, Allie thinks. And I...am the queen!

When the Watsons' lesson ends, she chats briefly with John Freeman, who is waiting for the new girl Candy to arrive. Then she goes over the Bronze program she's spent much of the week meticulously preparing. She retraces some of her handwriting, which could pass for type. Each of the dances Joe will learn—cha cha, tango, waltz, the other standards, along with a more ambitious paso doble and a romantic bolero she's added just for him—is described in glamorous terms and highlighted in the margins with smiling faces and dancer decals. At the bottom of the last page she's inscribed "LET'S DO IT!!!" in bulging bold letters.

Candy rushes in, late again, and escorts John onto the floor by the arm. He doesn't seem to mind that she's late, but this was a big mistake on Candy's part, because they are trying John for Medley today. Rob has yet to reprimand her for her repeated tardiness, so Allie makes a mental note to speak to him about it. Joe must be running late too, which is not unusual. He doesn't answer when she calls, but he may just be stuck in traffic. In the meantime, so as not to look too anxious, she decides to work alone in the practice room on the showcase she'll be doing with her most challenging student, Reggie Morris.

As she runs through the first part of the routine, she peeks at Candy and tries to evaluate her with the eye of an owner's wife. Candy's been there less than a month, she teaches only beginners and doesn't dance very well yet herself. Each day she takes a lesson from Rob. Still, she has a fluid way about her that shows potential. Her student is obviously infatuated; he doesn't care about the dancing. He's shy, you can see that, but he can't keep his eyes off her. And she is attractive, with long brunette hair, full lips, a well-proportioned figure, even if it is on the plump side. Of course, beauty only goes so far in this business. You might sell a beginner's program or even a Medley package on romance, but nobody's going to spend ten or fifteen thousand dollars on Bronze just to dance with you no matter how good looking you are. You have to sell the feeling. Rob was so right about that. And now here he is, leaving Mrs. Shapiro alone to practice her steps. He'll help Candy because he thinks just like I do. They demonstrate the fox trot together. Smart. John watches and smiles. He can't do it that smoothly, of course he can't. Rob puts him at ease with a joke and some encouraging remarks (God, he's good) and then returns to Mrs. Shapiro, leaving Candy beaming and feeling more graceful than she is and more confident with her student, who wishes he could move like she and Rob did, although he is too green to see the vast difference between the two. Candy will never inspire people like that, but then who can? Rob is the master.

"Where is he?" Rob says, popping his head into the practice room.

"I called but there was no answer. I left—" but Rob lets the door shut without listening to her finish, "—a message," she says, to herself.

She knows Rob is disappointed, but what can she do? Practice her routine, that's what. Always be making yourself better. Rule 7. Joe will be there, he's only fifteen minutes late. So she turns on the music and practices like the winner she is.

Half-way into the first run-through, she forgets the turn and backs into a cross-over at the wrong moment. She repeats the whole sequence. During the split, she catches sight of the other instructors again. Andrew has arrived and is practicing alone the tango he's prepared for Mrs. Kurtz that is too difficult for them both. Kristina teaches a small group of Silver members. Patti is all cleavage changing into her dance shoes, while Sean mans the music booth pretending not to notice. Allie spins as though Reggie is there and has led her into a turn. When she stops abruptly, as the routine demands, she observes Candy and John holding each other in dance position, just standing there giggling. *That cunt.* What time is it?

She does the whole routine again and messes up again, distracted about Joe. Even if he doesn't show up, he'll be at the club party on Friday. All they need to do is get him in the room; he feels the magic, she knows this, and Rob is such a good closer. Everything will be okay.

She runs through the routine again and stumbles in the same place.

You can bet this student of Candy's will be at the party, to see Candy again. And I'm sure Candy will be at the staff party afterward at our house. I wish Rob hadn't done that, I'm not ready to play hostess yet. When it was just his house when we were dating, before all the mess that followed, he hosted that party and we ended up playing Suck-and-Blow all night, passing the playing cards mouth-to-mouth. How filthy! This time I'll make a dance tape, just swing and Latin. He sits next to busty Annabelle (thank God she's gone) and sucks and blows with her all night, retrieving fallen cards from her cleavage, and thinks it's okay because I'm between that pimply short-timer—what was his name?—and Andrew! Christ. This time no games.

Over and over she dances the sequence she's bungled until she has it down pat, and commits to come in Saturday to practice the whole number until it's flawless. Joe's a half hour late. *He'd better be in an accident, that hairless pig.* He's not coming, she knows this. They'll have to try him Friday night. He's more likely to buy at a party anyway—he'll be in a great mood! She decides to call him one more time. In the music booth, her cell is at her ear when Rob pokes his head in.

"Don't bother. He called and cancelled."

She lowers the phone and feels like she should apologize. Before she can say anything, Candy approaches with her student by her side.

"Rob, do you have a minute?" she says. "John would like to talk to you about the benefits of signing up on our Medley program."

"Oh, terrific. John, is it? Let's see." He scans the room as though genuinely considering where to take them, and finally points to his right and says "No one's in here" before leading them into the only room ever used for closing. Allie can hear them laughing through the door and thinks: I will have my turn Friday.

*   *   *

After the party they pull up to their house having not spoken for miles. In the garage, Allie says his name just as he slams the door but he must not have heard her, because he goes inside without responding, leaving her in the car alone. Inside, she wipes the kitchen island and helps silently empty snack bags into bowls. "You know, I've been thinking," she says finally, after clearing her throat. "Joe might not have the money after all. He might have been telling the truth."

Rob removes from the tabletop a thick, cubicle glass vase that she bought at an estate sale on a recent spree. He was upset when she brought it home, along with a vintage breakfast platter and another much larger amphora-shaped vase that she's been filling with corks as they go through bottles of wine. "It's possible," Rob says wryly, setting the vase on the counter at arms' length like he's returning someone else's hysterical baby. "I suppose."

Anticipating his needs, she uncorks a bottle of Chardonnay. The alcohol-free club party had a low turnout, and that, along with Joe Stevens' refusal to purchase any portion of the Bronze, has put him in a sour mood.

"He has two more lessons. We can try him again—"

"No," Rob interrupts. "We lost him. Anyway, that new kid—what's his name? The one who signed onto Medley this week."

She accidentally brushes an empty glass with her elbow but catches it before it hits the floor. "John," she says.

"Nice grab. He seemed to be having a good time."

Allie helped Candy a lot by dancing with John at the party, demonstrating heel-toe, which he hadn't been taught yet, getting him to bend his knees, putting his mind on the dancing instead of on Candy.

She tries to crack ice into a bucket but several cubes fall to the floor. Instead of picking them up she backs onto a stool, rubs her hands through her hair and suddenly feels like crying. Rob pours them both a glass of wine and sits next to her.

He rubs her neck. "Do you remember Rule number 4?" he asks, after a long silence.

She doesn't know immediately what he means. She's read much of the book herself, or leafed through it, and Rob has repeated rules to her from time to time, but sometimes he amends the rules to match his own notions of success or satisfy his emotional prejudices. She can't always keep track, and now she looks at him searchingly. As always, an answer appears poised just beyond the surface of his eyes.

"You remember," he urges.

"Put—" she offers, hesitantly.

"The past behind you," he finishes for her. "Yes. Yes! Live in the now! Doesn't that make sense?"

She nods.

"We put our failures behind us and move forward." He kisses the top her head. "I'm going to get changed, they'll be here soon."

She follows him into the living room. "You don't think I could have done anything different? With Joe, I mean."

"Honey," he says, turning on the radio. "Inside, Joe knows he lost something tonight. It's his loss. We learn from it and we put our failures behind us. Right?"

"Right," she says, forcing a smile.

"Now let's put on our party mood," he says, adding on his way upstairs, "Someday we're going to be just as big as Ben."

While he's upstairs she drinks her wine and moves the couch to create space for dancing. He's right, of course: history is his story (one of Rob's sayings). Before he comes down, she eats half a bowl of potato chips to make up for the cold cuts and crudités she missed while they were in the office trying to close on Joe Stevens. She's starting to feel better.

Patti arrives first followed by Rick Caputo. Soon the entire staff of twelve is there and her mood turns upbeat after she puts on her favorite playlist. Greg protests at first that he dances for a living and doesn't want any part of it when he's off work, but he's pooh-poohed by the others and within a drink or two is dancing as uninhibitedly as the rest.

"I wonder if a porn star has sex when he's not performing," Travis jokes during a break in the music. Before Allie can find the song she wants, Rob, a little drunk by now on his third glass of wine, gets everyone's attention. "Listen up, everybody. . . Let me take this opportunity to announce our big sales this week. Candy, as many of you know, signed up her first Medley student the other night."

Spirited applause elicits an obliging curtsy from its honoree. "John—Freeman, is it?—is now a member. Candy is doing a wonderful job of showing him the benefits we provide." He raises his glass in her direction.

"He sees the benefits all right," Greg says to Sean, but loud enough that Allie can hear. *The lecher.*

She uncorks another bottle of wine. For one jaundiced moment the words *Candy* and *whore* unscramble in her head, only to scramble again instantly and vanish.

"And Rick sold another double showcase to the Forsythes," Rob continues. Rick, a veteran of foreign dance wars, as he puts it, having moved to the London club after starting with Ben here, came to work for Rob, the up-and-comer, on his return to the States. He sells so many programs it's taken for granted his students will continue and upgrade. He's also the best dancer at the club besides Rob, whose little speech ends in a cul-de-sac, leaving everyone quiet. The absence of what could have been raves for a sale to Joe Stevens leaves a hole in Allie's stomach. But after restarting the music, she shakes it off and pulls Rick onto the floor to get the ball rolling again, and maybe to show off in front of Candy, who looks a little too proud of herself next to Rob by the kitchen doorway.

It's a mambo: "Mambo Italiano"! Not a dance for beginners. *Eat that, Candy.* Allie's been working on her Latins for an instructor routine she'll perform at the showcase with Rob. Rick immediately gets her spinning. When she first started working at the club, before she was with Rob, she slept with Rick. Just once. Everyone learned about it. But because he's a notorious hound the backlash was minimal, unlike with Michel, or Noah, whose departures following their brief affairs with her inspired an unflattering chain of gossip.

Rick pushes her away and then reels her in with one hand before reversing her direction unexpectedly by hooking her hip with his raised lower leg. The others stop dancing and egg them on.

He was an original in bed too, she remembers that. For a time she had dreams about it, in which in addition to sex she found herself eating or preparing Italian deserts, like ricotta cheesecake and tiramisu. She's reminded of that as they finish the mambo with him extending her back over his arm to form a conjoined human arch. Amid playfully exaggerated whooping and hollering, she looks to see if Candy is paying attention. The upside down kitchen is empty. Rick straightens her up and bows dramatically. She remains standing.

"Where is Robby?" she asks no one in particular.

The bathroom is vacant and no one is on the patio when she checks.

"Has anyone seen Rob?" she repeats on her return. The music has stopped, and the others are talking and ignore her. Sean suggests they play a game.

"How about Suck-and-Blow?" Greg offers immediately.

"No!" Allie cries. "No Suck-and-Blow."

"What's Suck-and-Blow?" Katrina asks.

"No Suck-and-Blow," Allie repeats. She opens and closes the door to the extra bedroom. "I'm trying to find Rob."

"Oh, come on, don't be a party pooper," Greg says. "Not everyone was here the last time."

"I mean it," she says, accompanied by a stern, this-is-my-house-now glare.

Kelly says, "I think I saw him go upstairs with Candy."

"Fine," says Greg, quick to adapt. "What about something else."

"I know a good game," Patti says. "It's called Psychiatrist."

Allie isn't listening. She calls Rob's name and then scurries up the stairs. The bedroom door is closed. "Rob, our guests want to play a game," she calls out before entering. The room is empty.

Downstairs, Patti is explaining to Greg. "I can't say until someone is chosen to be 'it.' That person has to figure out the rules."

When Allie returns, Greg tells her, "Allie, you're it—for nixing our Suck-and-Blow."

"Shut up, I can't find Robby," she says, with unintended ferocity. She's a little dizzy from her second glass of wine but goes to the kitchen to pour another one anyway. It's there that she smells smoke.

"Honey," Rob splutters when she opens the door to the garage. He steps away clumsily from his position by the workbench, several inches from Candy.

"You caught me," he says vaguely, and then holding up a cigarette adds, "Only my second one today" before putting it out in a flower pot.

"I should have stopped him," Candy says. She is also smoking.

"Yes, you should have."

Allie notices two of the fluorescent lights in the ceiling fixtures flickering. "They want to play a game," she says after a pregnant silence.

"Great! Good, let's play a game." He squeezes between her and the car. "You can finish that inside if you want," he says to Candy from the door. "If that's all right with you, hon."

Allie doesn't speak or turn. "No, that's okay," Candy says, putting her cigarette out. "I'll live longer without it, right?" She laughs nervously as she pockets a book of matches from the workbench that Allie, alone after she and Rob have gone inside, noticed were from Mama Stuffiti's.

"Everyone sits in a semi-circle like they are now except Allie. She stands in the middle and asks questions," Patti explains to everyone while Allie waits upstairs. "She can ask anything of anyone as long as it's about that person. But instead of answering for themselves, whoever she asks will answer for the person sitting to their left. Allie won't know this; she'll have to figure it out. So, if she asks Greg, I don't know—'Are you wearing a blue shirt?'—even though he is wearing a blue shirt, he will say—?"

"No," Greg says.

"Right. Because Kristina, on his left, is not wearing a blue shirt. But, if he wants to—and here's the key—he can lie and answer yes, in which case Kristina says 'Psychiatrist.' Whenever anyone says 'Psychiatrist' everyone gets up and sits somewhere else, with someone new on their left."

"I don't get it," Kristina says. "Why do I say 'Psychiatrist'?"

"That's what you say when the person answering the question answers incorrectly, as it applies to you. If they answer correctly, you don't say anything, and the game goes on: Allie asks someone else a new question. But if they answer incorrectly, you say 'Psychiatrist.' They might answer wrong on purpose or because they don't know the right answer for you, but either way, you say 'Psychiatrist.' 'Psychiatrist' is just the name. It could be called 'Eggplant' or 'Sapphire' or whatever, but it's not."

"She'll get it right away," Candy says.

"Well, maybe, but you try to fool her, that's the thing. Don't be obvious. Oh, and we should encourage her to ask personal questions—sexual questions, or whatever. Instead of 'What are you wearing?' something like, 'Have you ever had sex in a public place?' or 'How many partners have you had in the last five years?' It's more fun that way."

In the bathroom upstairs, Allie is throwing up potato chips. When she finishes, she sits on the lid, confused and light-headed. He'd been having a couple drinks after work with Ben, he told her two weeks ago Monday—on business. And there was another night, allegedly with Ben, when Rob had tiptoed in while she was half asleep. Allie remembers meeting Rob's first wife when she was still in the business, an extraordinary dancer, elegant, much closer to Rob's age, and her parting words whispered tellingly at the showcase in that dazzling hotel ballroom in Denver: Keep a close eye on him, honey. Of course Allie had heard the rumors. If they were true, she would change him, that's how determined she was. She had changed him. His consent to wed after a year of dating was an admission of change, he who had vowed never to marry again. He told her that. He assured her his willingness to marry was about more than just the baby. And when she later lost it he was the one who insisted on going through with the wedding, already planned for the weekend of his family reunion.

She examines her pale complexion in the mirror. She had changed him. He was smoking a cigarette, that's all she saw. Everything else could be explained. When she hears her name, she splashes water on her face and joins the others, self-assured.

"Just ask anything to begin with," Patti advises. "When you get the hang of it, you can be a little bolder."

Rob has mixed a pitcher of Sangrias and is walking around the sectional pouring everyone a drink. Once he settles in, Allie begins by asking Andrew how long he's been in the business. "Thirty years" is Andrew's response, an obvious falsehood. On his left, Patti says "Psychiatrist" and everyone changes places.

"It's simple," Allie says. "You don't answer the question honestly." Patti tells her that's not it, and to continue.

Allie asks Rick who his favorite student is, knowing that he, like Rob, favors Heather Lamb. Rick answers honestly, but then Kristina, seated next to him, says "Psychiatrist" and they all move again.

Allie pours herself a drink from the pitcher of Sangrias. Sean does a spot-on impersonation of Rick rumbaing eye-to-eye with Heather Lamb unrelated to the game—at least Allie assumes it's unrelated. When she asks the next question, nobody says "Psychiatrist." Maybe it's not *what* they answer but *the way they answer*, she thinks.

She asks more questions. Rob replenishes drinks after everyone changes places for the third time. Allie thinks: Sometimes they tell the truth, other times they lie; sometimes they get up and move, and sometimes they don't. Once in a while someone says "Psychiatrist," but just as often they remain silent. She notices Suzanne can't stop eating snack food and wonders if it is part of the game. They change places after a lie, she notes, but not always—they move after the truth sometimes too. Where do they move to? *Damn it!* She hasn't paid any attention to that. Now she's really confused.

"Don't be such a prude, Allie," Greg says, after they'd been playing the game for half an hour. "Open it up a little."

Everyone is laughing and having a good time except her. She tries to play along, to act the good hostess despite everything. Rule 6: Don't be afraid to step out of your comfort zone. She asks Kristina when she lost her virginity, Andrew how many men he's slept with. His response—fewer than fifty—evokes a self-congratulatory chuckle from Travis, to his left, "Psychiatrist," and then howls of laughter as everyone changes places again. Allie's frustration escalates with each round. Why doesn't Rob sense her alienation and come to her aid? She is sure that he and the others are laughing at her now for failing to crack the code.

Think! Allie. The person next to the one I question sometimes says "Psychiatrist." When?

To be funny, she asks Sean, who is straight, if he would consider sleeping with Matthew McConaughey. He makes a big show, stating that although Mr. McConaughey is a gorgeous, rich movie star, he, Sean, is so happy with his mate he would never consider cheating, even with him. Kelly, on his left, busts up the room when she takes the bait and says "Psychiatrist," and again they all switch places.

Allie has a revelation: they are answering for the person on their left! Rob and Candy are seated next to one another now. Everyone is still laughing, and Candy, nearly convulsive, falls halfway into Rob's lap.

Blurt it out! Allie thinks. Get the game over with! They are answering for the person on their left, and . . . when they answer wrong the person says "Psychiatrist." That's it!

Before she can say anything, she thinks she hears someone mutter the name Joe Stevens and spins around. They are laughing at her. Is it Patti mocking her recent failure? *Or that jealous bitch, Kelly?* She might have imagined it. She looks to Rob's face for answers and finds it red with mirth. He bends forward to put down his drink as a hand lands on his right knee.

"Candy!" Allie says the name so loudly the room goes quiet. For a moment she isn't sure what to say or why she shouted. Then she remembers.

"Have you ever slept with the person sitting to your right?"

"Whoa," Greg says. He is seated to Candy's right but understands, as everyone, especially Allie, does that Candy will be answering for Rob, to her left, and that the question is posed to determine if the two have been having an affair. The grandfather clock in the hallway strikes one. A strap on Allie's blouse slips off, exposing her bony shoulder. Candy looks directly at her, and to give Rob an easy way out by remaining silent, lies. "No," she says, without flinching. Allie doesn't blink either. She rotates her head just enough to observe her husband with the singular desperation of an impossible, contradictory appeal: Don't say anything, her face pleads, my love, my life—but be honest! A cold glare is all he offers in return. Fine. Good. Silence is good. But just when she believes she's survived, Rob opens his big mouth.

"Psychiatrist."

Immediately he feigns confusion—he'd misspoken, had failed to understand—but it's too late. No one moves, even though the rules of the game demand it. They all fidget or sip their drinks without making eye contact with anyone. There. There are your facts, idiot! Allie thinks. They did it. Everyone knows about it. And you're a fool.

Candy sinks deep into the cushions. Greg stands up first, not to change seats— the game is over—but with a consoling hand extended toward Allie, who trembling and half-encircled appears more isolated than ever. She stares at Rob, her hands crisscrossed over her chest, gripping her upper arms, until Greg touches her shoulder, at which point she flees the house that no longer feels like her own.

"I told you we should have played Suck-and-Blow," Greg says, but no one even smiles. Rob rises with a sigh and heads after her.

* * *

The parquet dance floor is surrounded by two dozen circular tables dressed in white tablecloths set for the evening's dinner. A pair of rectangular tables topped with ribbons and trophies stand behind a microphoned podium, where the master of ceremonies is often interrupted or replaced altogether by Ben Carlson, at his discretion. Above the stage, by an exceptionally thin cable, hangs an ornate chandelier that aptly reflects the stylized ritual taking place below.

Allie stands at the edge of the dance floor with her student, Reggie Morris. She is the only one from her club not cheering for Andrew and Mrs. Kurtz as he leads her through steps barely recognizable as tango. Instead, she replays the events preceding her decision thirty-six hours earlier to give Rob another chance. He'd caught her in her car outside the house and they drove to a forest preserve where she cried and listened to his excuses. He admitted his betrayal. He pleaded for forgiveness, promising to be true and to fire Candy, who, to be fair to everyone, he would steer to Ben Carlson for an interview. Back at the house, where the party had broken up, she maintained her distrust and resistance. But Rob was determined to make it up, and somehow they ended up in bed. The sex was rough, a pantomime of repressed anger. She scratched his back, he bit her neck in retaliation, hard enough to leave a mark. Later that morning she awoke by herself, unable to move. Her period had begun, and she was aware that her feelings toward Rob were not unlike hatred. Now, across the room, he complements Ben, the aspirant at his mentor's side, pretending as he watches Andrew fumble through his routine to be proud and impressed, although she knows he's been considering firing him. Rob is taller than Ben, and striking in black tie and tails, his confidence limited only by its relation to his neighbor's. Older and much richer, Ben's self-satisfied manner is absolute. Without waiting for the routine to end, he directs Rob into the lobby.

Recalling Friday night's scene, Allie wonders if she will ever live down the humiliation. She has spoken no more than she has to to her club mates, occupying her mind by going over her routines. Her dress, a cobalt blue number with a slit-cut and spangles that Rob bought her with this event in mind, has generated only one compliment, and that from Joe Stevens, with whom she was very curt. No money for a showcase or a portion of the Bronze, yet he shows up to watch and get the last dollar's value from his expiring limited membership. *Pig. With that beer belly, no wonder you're alone.* As she got ready before leaving the house, she decided a proper tribute to her husband, one he deserved, was to maximize the effect of the dress by leaving her undergarments behind.

She and Reggie are to follow Kelly, who spins onto the floor at her student's lead. Their paso doble opens dramatically. Through the open double doors across the room she can see Ben and Rob in the lobby conferring in private. Following a brief exchange, they shake hands as ceremonial smiles slither across their faces that from a distance blur the thin line between them. Something has happened and Allie knows what it is. He walks even taller, Rob does, when he reenters the ballroom. Ben remains at the doorway overseeing the fruits of his life's labor. Rob stops to watch the routine, grinning uncontrollably, an embodiment of ambition realized. Before it ends, he crosses the room, unable to restrain himself, allowing her to see him smile broadly although he knows it is too soon after their reconciliation to express joy, that it undermines his profession of shame. Allie can sense his dilemma. In that instant she recognizes how all that has happened between them in the last two years has been like action in a play whose long run is coming to an end, a play in which Rob is the promising supporting actor and she is a replaceable young extra. Something has happened, she knows what it is alright, and he can remove his make-up now and savor the success of his performance before preparing for his next role, the first of many starring ones.

"He's letting us go," he says softly, so that Reggie won't hear. "Ben is." She can see how difficult it is for him to play it cool, she can still admire his control, knowing how badly he wants to rejoice, to broadcast his triumph.

"He just agreed to it. With the terms we talked about."

"You're kidding," Allie says. "That's wonderful." She is certain now that she hates him.

Kelly's routine ends thunderously, a real crowd-pleaser. Reggie cannot stop fidgeting. She reaches for his hand. "We're up. It'll be okay." Even though she was unable to practice the day before like she'd planned, having been up all night with Rob, she knows she can back-lead Reggie through the performance if he falters.

Rob leans closer as the crowd applauds: "This is what I always wanted," he says. "My independence."

When the clapping dies out, Ben Carlson is at the microphone, repeating the names of the previous dancers and introducing the next routine.

"—from our Metro East club here in town, Reggie Morris and his instructor Allie Martin will perform a cha-cha."

The dance is simple. She choreographed it to suit Reggie's limited abilities. She watches him closely so she can help him recover from any inevitable missteps. At the same time, she remains conscious of Ben Carlson, who has receded from the podium to the entranceway where a blonde-haired woman in street clothes is greeting him coyly. Double-spun to the edge of the dance floor, Allie loses sight of them. There Joe Stevens looks on, his arms crossed, resting on his fat belly. Too late for you, mister, Allie thinks. *Cheapskate. Loser.*

Rejoining her, Reggie steps immediately into fifth position. In the same moment she tries to back-lead him into a cross-over. Was that right? No, Reggie was right! A quick spin disguises her mistake, but there is Rob, in front of her when she twirls, alone, independent (*the bastard*), with a disapproving glare that halts her like a wrench thrust between interlocking gears.

She stumbles on the edge of the dance floor and falls to one knee. It is Candy she recognizes in that instant, the one speaking to Ben by the door. She has dyed her hair blonde. They stop talking when Allie falls, reacting instinctively to the audience's sympathetic groans. Reggie freezes, helpless and terrified. She gets up quickly and finds a place in the music to pick it up again, leading him back, trying to will away her mistake, and his fear and disappointment.

Then she sees Greg suppressing a laugh. Always invisible giggles from this guy. Another turn, with Rob eyeing them anxiously. A stillness underscores the scene as Reggie, whom she also despises now (if he could lead, this wouldn't have happened!), raises one arm to turn her again, remembering to hold his hand rigid. She's taught him well, *the clod*, although even with his hand held properly, their arms raised as one, she manages to free herself with a slick maneuver for a final sequence of her own spontaneous design.

Rob and Greg she knows will recognize this instantly. Ben and Candy, Joe Stevens, the others are not aware of her extemporizing until they notice Reggie shuffle stupidly and then stop altogether and watch dumb like the others—watch Allie spin three, four, five times, and persist in spinning even after Rob has motioned to the sound man to cut the music. No one knows what is happening. The first words spoken, by Rob—That's enough—do not reach their target, but instead rise and dissipate in the otherwise hushed ballroom like the smoke from one of his squelched-out cigarettes. Ben Carlson abandons Candy as the whirling continues. Allie adds an unexpected twist she considers timely, even artful—a deft unzipping of her new dress, which falls limply to the floor. It spins with her, tangled in her feet as Rob rushes forward, his previous euphoria displaced by a stunned and embarrassed rage. Ben likewise darts in her direction. He and Rob remove their tuxedo jackets as they advance, to stifle her mad, endless spinning, to cover her emaciated bare body.

This is me naked, she thinks, as they descend upon her, jackets raised, like two outraged Draculas. *Raw meat on a spit*, is how she imagines it first. *A human corkscrew. . . a child's top. . . an egg beater. . .* as her ideas about herself begin to rapidly unwind.

RUBIES
LEONARD KRESS

I've always loved rubies. Ever since I was a child. It's not just the fact that Ruby is my name and that rubies are my birthstone. It also has something to do with growing up in northeast Iowa and all that *Wizard of Oz* crap that everyone else seems to think so much of—*If happy little bluebirds fly beyond the rainbow, why oh why can't I...?* Not emeralds like you might expect, but rubies, ruby slippers, the ones that Dorothy lifted from the dead witch's feet. It doesn't matter that this took place in Kansas, and I live in Iowa; even here we tend to confuse the two states.

But people hated that movie. There was always a big to-do whenever it showed on TV, and the local video stores even kept it behind the counter as if it were some sort of porno flick.

I don't know that much about the politics behind it, but I do know that it had a lot to do with all the witches and magic in the movie and how all that interfered with lessons parents were trying to teach their kids about Jesus. To them, it was just another Hollywood product trying to get their kids hooked on Satan. That was reason enough, though, to attract teenagers, and for a time when I was in Junior High, there were even unmarked bootlegged editions of the video circulating throughout the school. One kid made a couple hundred dollars selling them out of her backpack. Anyway, that's what I heard.

At least we had twisters, lots of them. My friends here never believe me, though, when I tell them I never saw one in person. Too busy rushing down into the cellar or filing out Indian-style to the hallway at school. I did have a great aunt whose baby was carried away by one, according to my mother. This was back in the forties when all the men were off at war. The sad part of it was that she was clinging to her newborn at the time but couldn't keep hold of her. My great aunt survived it, though, and went on to have six more kids. By the time I met her, she was already in a nursing home, suffering from Alzheimer's, so she didn't remember a thing about it. I really wanted to ask her what it felt like watching your baby spiral up over the house and barn, up over the poplars, watching it get smaller and smaller, till it was barely the size of a fertilized egg, before disappearing altogether. I was named after her—not my aunt, of course, but the infant, whose body they never found.

So you can see why rubies are really important to me. That's why I'm shopping for them now, though it's taken me an awful long time to get one. It's taken till my second husband and the birth of my daughter Stacey (short for Anastasia) to get one. Actually Stacy is my second daughter, too. The first one—and here I'm guessing it was a little girl and not a little boy—was aborted. It was just after I got married the first time, right out of high school, and you'd think that since I didn't get pregnant till *after* the ceremony, we should have kept it and raised it. But my husband would have nothing of it. He wanted to go to Chicago, just the two of us, me getting a job as a waitress or something and him trying to work his way into the Art Institute. He really believed that his baling-wire sculptures would take him places, and he surely had me convinced at the time. I still have nightmares about that Ob-Gyn in Madison, Wisconsin, who performed the procedure. In them, he's coming at me, and all I can see under his surgical mask and hat are his big dark eyes flashing under bushy eyebrows waving like tendrils of wheat whipped up by a prairie wind. He's holding a long piece of baling wire and commanding me to spread my legs and stick my heels into the stirrups. I know that he's planning to stick that wire with all those barbs up inside me, scraping it against my uterus, hoping that one of those barbs will snag on my precious ruby so he can pluck it out.

BIRTHDAY POEM WITH NERVOUS DOG
SCOTT BEAL

Last night the sky banged boulders for sparks.
The clouds lit themselves on fire and set off
the sprinklers. A deep bass laser light show
to ring in your new year while you slept.
The dog got caught in it and came in shaking.
That dog hates clash. That dog barks at doorbells
on TV and yesterday trawled a jawful of candy
from a bag left in reach. She made a gooey trail
of wrappers across the floor. I love our old dog
but not as well as some people love their dogs.
I engage in basic maintenance. Open the door
when she stands there whining. Top off her bowls
twice a day. Or send the kids. The dog's been
with us most of our married life and I go days
without touching it, take your pick, the life
or the dog, but last night she came in shaking
because the world made all the sounds of ripping
itself apart, and I wrapped around her soaking coat
and shook with her. You were asleep. I whispered
It's okay, Muddy, it's okay. Nothing you say
will convince a dog these are the same explosions
that come eight times each spring. The dog's name
is Muddy Waters. We named her after the blues,
not because we looked at this flinching furball
and thought, she's part of our lives that's going to die.
But she's part of our lives that's going to die.
She is a nexus of routines and gestures so ingrained
we'll have to remind ourselves several times each day
to no longer make them. She's a silly hunger
for a jumble of sickening lures. She is humming tissue.
She roars at the knocking door and lays herself down
like a dam at the foot of the children's bed.
People say it's hard to be married, but it's hard
to be anything. Holes get punched in the ceiling

where our warmth rises to collect.
We're going to lose so much. The flashing sky
doesn't impress me. I'm going to learn
who you are all over again.

MEMORIAL DAY
SCOTT BEAL

The day that ended in the thin thread of our marriage
snapping off in her teeth, two girls splashed
by the dock in waves from jet ski wakes.
Grills smoked. Frisbees whizzed. The swan family was found
through binoculars to have lost another gray cygnet.
Eight bocce balls gleamed in the grass, nicked green and red,
unplayable now that the yellow jack bounced
into the lake and was taken by the fish out past the dropoff
and lowered into their trove of lost human things,
car keys and corkscrews, earrings and watches,
years of objects knocked overboard. Before stashing
the jack, as they do with each thing, the fish, dozens
small as your palm, tasted it with their lips,
the way some have tasted hooks and fingers removing hooks,
the way some have tasted bread crumbs tossed by the hands
of those two girls, an astonishing swarm flashing
around the dock for as long as it takes to tear apart
a loaf—these fish opened their lips one after another
against the small yellow globe and found it hard,
inedible, and pushed it kiss by kiss down to the deep.

That is one story, and I believe it. But tracing the day
back further one finds the turtle we drove past before turning
in the driveway. One finds the car behind us that failed
to see or stop, fat tires that slammed across its shell
without cracking or killing it, and the way a man stood
in the road to wave other cars around it as we left
our daughters staring from the edge of the drive.
One of us found a strip of cardboard and held it
before the stunned beast's snapping beak, tempting
and prodding until it sprang and clamped with force enough
to break bone. We dragged it, jaws locked,
over the lip of a plastic tub and carried it between us
down to the boat launch. It was heavy and angry

and we worked in a hurry. We overturned the tub
into the shallows and watched as the turtle floundered,
righted itself, and jetted away, dark head
cutting the surface in the direction of the swans.

A FOREIGN LANGUAGE
BEN HOFFMAN

At first I think the man at the coffee shop is speaking a foreign language. Something from one of those lost East European tribes submerged under communism that only recently reappeared, like species you read about but don't truly believe are still kicking. But I listen closely behind my classifieds and it is pure gibberish. We are in the plush chairs in the middle. I take a peek. A giant babbling bald man resting a coffee on his slouching stomach. He is alone. No phone, no bluetooth. He seems to be speaking to his coffee. No one else notices. People are doing their own coffee shop things. Crosswording. Phone playing. Leaning in to hear a lover.

The man is deep in discussion with his coffee. Maybe telling it not to spill. Stay right there while I tell you about the people who have left me. He is stroking it as if it is a beard. His shirt is coffee-stained, like this has gone awry before. I feel bad for him, in the way you do for crazy people who don't have families or friends or jobs. Then I think how I don't have those things and I didn't need to be crazy to not have them. I want to tell this man he can lose everything without being crazy. You don't need to invent imaginary friends or languages. Just be normal but not quite as good as everyone else.

I cannot say this to the man because I do not speak his language. I often feel this way but here it is literally true. I wish the man were speaking German, because even though I do not know much German, I know a German word that only Germans have that this man might like. The word describes the feeling of being alone in a forest, which is a place I have never been alone.

*   *   *

There are a few things I am good at. I am good at noticing. I am good at feeling bad for people. These are skills that ought to serve me well but I cannot see that they've gotten me anywhere. I am most good at making people nervous. I can do that better than anyone. This is a skill that ought to hurt, and it has hurt me.

I want to tell the strange man that I am impressed. He is doing something better than anyone else. I put down my classifieds. I speak gibberish to him, mumble consonants and vowels. He looks at me like I have slapped him out of a dream. He shouts, What the hell are you doing? People stop their coffee shop things to look at me. You would think they would look at the shouting man but they look at me. This man, the man shouts. This man is trying to talk to me! You would think his coffee would spill during his yelling but it stays upright on his stomach as if glued. You would think other people would notice this, but only I do. I want to ask him about this balancing trick but it is too late for that. Sorry, I say. I am very sorry.

I have made the barista nervous. Baristas get nervous when someone like me is in their coffee shop. This applies to waiters in restaurants, salespeople in shops, drivers in taxis, everyone who has a place. The barista cannot focus. He messes up a drink. A lady in scarves yells at him about foam. We are alike, I want to tell the barista. I am also nervous. I also mess up. Maybe soon you will lose your job and we can be even more alike. It is every bit as bad as it seems. I will show you the ropes.

I want to hug him. I get up from my chair but when I approach the bar the barista is done redoing the foam. He is taking change from a beautiful man, their hands finding the right space, skimming as close as possible without touching, navigating like little planes. I would need a control tower for this sort of precision. Meanwhile a child has taken my plush chair. The child is eating cookies and the man does a funny thing. He reaches out to take a cookie, but instead he brushes some crumbs from the child's collar to the floor. I leave the coffee shop but out in the world it is impossibly sunny. People are looking at jewelry in windows, turning right on red, wrapping each other in their arms with the proper amount of force, like they have all been practicing, like they are symphony and I am audience.

GICHIGAMI
LINDSEY STEFFES

There's a dip in the island and right between two ancient firs, my house grows like a weed. Dad's a carpenter, and he's been laid off for the winter. Keeps making add-ons to the top floor so our house looks just like a birthday cake. Snow like the icing and all.

"Easy on the left side," I tell him. "I think it's going to tip."

So he throws a few more bricks onto the chimney.

"Balance things out," he says.

And he keeps going like that, adding rooms and bricks until the chimney reaches right up to the sky. Until the smoke becomes the clouds because you can't see where one starts and the other stops.

Come springtime, our house is going to be a castle. We're going to tower above the whole island. As tall as the lighthouse. They'll have to get a ladder just to ring our bell. A pulley for the mailman.

"Something right out of the movies," Dad says.

"What color?" he asks me, because I'll be queen.

"Blue," I tell him. "Blue as you can get it. Blue like the ocean."

"Never seen the ocean," Dad says. "Just the lake." And I tell him to check a postcard.

"When I get back, there better be gulls," I say, but he doesn't laugh.

I pull on Dad's rubber boots. Wrap duct tape around the soles to keep out the snow. It's like the Tundra out there. I don't know where that is, but that's what the weatherman says and the news anchors all joke about it.

"You need a coat," Dad says. "In there."

I open the closet and rifle through jackets. I know what I'm looking for. Musk. Lilac. Two black, marble eyes staring up from the collar. I find Mom's mink coat and wrap it around me. Dig my fingers into the pockets and pull out a couple mothballs.

"Not that one," he says. "Not today."

"What difference does it make?"

Dad folds his shoulders. I can tell he doesn't want to fight.

"Besides," I say. "I look good. Really good." I think about the mainland kids, the native boys in junior high. Wish they could see me like this.

"Whatever you say," Dad says.

"Don't wait up."

"Be careful on the road." Dad says that every time, because the road is long and because it's made of ice. In the summertime, we take the ferry from our island to the mainland, but in the winter the whole lake freezes over. And then we've got a road. Tourists come all the way up here just to take pictures of it. Just to take a step on the ice. Just to say they did it.

I have to do it every day because school's on the mainland, along with everything else. The island's only got me, Dad, a couple neighbors and the lighthouse. Half the time, nobody's even manning it.

"I'll be fine," I tell Dad.

I leave the castle, and right away, I can feel the cold setting in. I let my hair down and wrap it around my neck like a scarf. Keep walking until I get to Onie's. About a mile and a half.

When I start crossing the lake, the wind picks up. Starts blowing the snow cross-wise so that everything's white and endless and all mixed together. The snow, ice, the sky. You can't tell up from down. I track the painted edge of the road so I don't get lost.

Last winter, a couple kids were coming across to the island, and they went off the road. Followed their own trail and never came back. The year before, it happened to a group of tourists, some backpackers all the way from Sweden. And years before, to a single woman, a local, who should've known better. Dad thinks they all probably fell through somewhere, but I think they just kept on walking. Maybe walked all the way to Canada.

"It's possible," I told him.

Dad pulled out a map. Traced a line across the lake.

"They'd only get to Michigan," he said. "And no one wants to go there."

By the time I get to the mainland, my hands are numb. Feels like they don't belong to me anymore. I can feel the stinging deep within my chest, and I wonder about how long it'd take for my body to freeze inside and out, just like the deer carcass Dad keeps in the garage.

I walk over the icy sand, past the row of beach bungalows, and look in on the tourists. Lights out in all but one. They've got a fire going, a good one. They've got kids on the floor playing board games. Peeking through the blinds.

Onie's is the third house, top floor. I stand at the door for a second. Fish for a comb beneath the mothballs, find one and run it through a couple times. Onie likes it neat. She likes things in order.

"Onie," I say, knocking. "Open up. I need a dress."

I can hear heavy footsteps crawling down the stairs. The wood bending and bowing under her heavy frame. After a few seconds, the door cracks open. I can see one bulging eye peering out.

"You've got eyes like a dinosaur," I tell her. "Like a robin's egg."

She swings the door out and lets me in.

"Hurry up," she says. "The cold."

I follow Onie up the stairs. Her bones creak like a coil spring mattress. She's over a hundred years old. A Red Cliff Native, here long before the ferry and the ice road and all the growlers, that's what they call our kind, the white people.

"Onie," I say.

She turns to me, lipstick crossing her jagged teeth.

"What's the dress for?" she asks me, but I don't want to say. She's got loose lips. She'll blab to somebody and somebody will tell Dad.

"Blue," I say. "Short hem. Sequins."

Onie nods.

"Don't you want to write that down?" I ask her, and she looks real offended.

"No," she tells me. She's got it. Says I should come back next week.

*　　*　　*

At Big Water, I drink a pop and watch the cook drop gulps of batter on the grill. The pancakes sprout up like daisies, full and golden. Makes me think of springtime. Still four months away.

"Want some?" Sylvia comes over and I say no. Just here to talk.

"Getting ready for the dance," I tell her.

"Why bother?" she says. "Your dad won't let you go."

"What does he know?"

"More than most men," Sylvia says. "You'd be surprised." I know she only says that because she's after him. She's been chasing Dad since junior high, along with all the other women on the mainland. All gossips, all trying to get in my ear. A real catch, they tell me. A prize. A house on the island, a full head of hair. I don't know what's so great about that.

"You should listen to your Daddy." Sylvia sits down next to me.

"I'm going to the dance."

Sylvia tosses her hair behind her shoulders. In the whole town, she's the only one with red hair. The natives think she's cursed. That she's trouble.

"You got a guy?"

I can feel the heat coming all at once. The burning blush. She can see it too.

"Who's the lucky guy?" she asks. "Which one? Tell me."

"Can't say," I answer. "You know him."

"Everyone knows everyone," she says. "Spill."

I blow bubbles in my pop.

"Are you gonna wear makeup? You should probably wear makeup," Sylvia tells me.

"How should I know?" I say.

I leave her a couple dollars, get up and leave. Now, I've got to go buy makeup.

At the grocery store, there's only one aisle with makeup, and it's way in the back because no one ever goes there. I sift through expired lipsticks, making colored streaks along my arm. Try to pick a color, but nothing looks right.

A couple girls from my class walk in. I yank the fur sleeve down to cover my rainbow wrist. Hide behind the aisle until their backs are turned, and rush out before they notice. Two colors, Velvet Tango and Orange Crush, tucked deep inside my pocket.

When I get back to the castle, there's a lady standing by our door. Probably another tourist. She's got nylons and a pink jacket. Looks just like a flamingo with her legs stuck two feet deep in the snow.

"What are you doing here?" I say.

She doesn't turn around. The lady keeps staring up at the castle like she wants to buy it. It's not for sale, I want to tell her. I don't know how many times I've had to say that. These people never understand.

She runs her fingers against the front door without rapping.

I walk closer.

"Hello?" I say. "Do you need something? I live here."

The lady takes off her cap and stands still. I watch her bright yellow hair move in the wind. After a few seconds, she turns around to face me. It's Mom.

The last time I saw her, she was packing her bags. Said she was going away.

"Will you be gone a long time?" I asked her. I was sitting on her bed, watching her iron each of her dresses. Watching her drape them over hangers and tuck them into a worn floral suitcase.

"I don't know why I bother ironing. The second I pack them up, they're wrinkled all over again."

"Then why don't you stop?"

She put the iron down. I thought she was listening, but then she started up again.

"My mother always ironed everything, and she tore me apart if my clothes weren't pressed," she told me. "I hated it, but now I'm the same as her. You will too someday."

"Iron everything?" I said. "I'll never do that."

"No, you'll be just like me."

"I don't want to be like you," I told her.

She pressed her lips together tightly.

"That's how it works."

The next day, Mom was gone before I woke up. Dad was tiling the kitchen like nothing happened. Didn't say a word about it.

And now, she's standing here in front of me, a tropical bird caught in the snow, a stupid smile across her face. Earrings to match her jacket like something from a department store. I used to think about her becoming one of those ladies, the kind that goes sightseeing with new clothes on and hair curled up in tiny waves.

"You look old," I tell her.

She looks down at the snow. Tries to unbury her feet.

"You look different," I say. "Those stockings."

She pulls at her nylons and smoothes out her skirt.

"Dad's been adding to the house," I tell her. "It's much bigger since you left. Prettier too."

Together we look up at the castle. My house, not hers.

"Are you going to say something?" I ask her. "Are you going to tell me where you've been?"

"Aren't you happy to see me?" she finally says. "You thought I was a stranger."

"You are a stranger," I answer because it's true and because I don't mind hurting her feelings.

Mom smiles, and trudges closer to me. She leans over and tucks my hair behind my ear. I almost pull away.

"Nice coat," she says. "Looks familiar."

I pull the fur coat tight.

"Does Dad know you're here?"

She shakes her head. "It's a surprise."

"Some surprise," I say. And she follows me inside.

When she walks in, it's like she never left. She sets her bags down in the hallway and goes right to the kitchen. Pulls out the teakettle.

"You want some?" she asks. "You like tea?"

"That's the sort of thing you should already know."

She puts the kettle on the stove.

When the tea's ready, we sit across from each other at Dad's new oak table. She doesn't say much. Just things about the snow, the weather.

Then she wanders through the castle, touching things: the carved banister, brand new, the maritime maps tacked up against the walls, Dad's row of rubber boots. She stops at each place, running her fingers along the edges and looking real close like she's checking for dust. I follow her through, watching. She is older. It shows in her face, in the way she walks and the way she holds herself.

We climb the stairs to the second floor, and she makes her way to Dad's bedroom.

"Looks just the same," she finally says.

"It's not the same," I tell her. "We've done a lot since you left."

"The knob on my vanity's still broken," she says. "It's just the same."

"Everything's different," I say. "We've got a third floor, we've got new rooms, new furniture. Dad says it's Victorian style, like in the movies."

Mom smiles.

"You didn't even see. You don't even know."

"It feels the same," she says.

"It's not the same." And I'm mad now. "Dad works everyday."

"The painting needs some work," she says. "Did you see that blue?"

"As blue as the ocean," I tell her.

"Why would you paint a house blue?" She's smiling that stupid smile, and I know she'll never understand.

"It's not your house," I say. "We don't care what you think."

She sits on Dad's bed, takes off her coat. Underneath, she's got this yellow, paisley dress on, bunching at the waist. She looks smaller than she did before. Tired, with too much makeup on. She sees me watching.

"I got you something," Mom says. She reaches in her pocket and pulls out a little box wrapped in white tissue paper. Hands it over.

"What is it?"

"Just open it," Mom says, so I do. I tear at the corners. Make sure to rip the tissue into tiny pieces so she knows I'm still angry. I open the lid, and a pressed flower falls from the box into my lap.

"A flower?" I ask her.

"It's an orange blossom," she says. "All the way from Florida, from my backyard."

I cup the flower in my hand and trace the small, white petals. Feel the wax between my fingertips. She leans closer to me.

"Isn't it beautiful?" Mom says. "I had my own orange tree. Fresh fruit every morning."

"We've got a fruit tree in our backyard," I tell her. "We've got cherries all summer."

"But those die in the wintertime. In Florida, those blossoms come year round," she says. "You'd love it."

"I'm never leaving the island," I say even though she's not asking. "I don't like the warm weather."

"That's not true," she says. Mom points to a framed picture on Dad's dresser.

"That's you as a baby," she tells me. "Our first vacation. Your father and I drove you all the way to Tennessee to see your grandma. You cried the whole way there, but the second we stepped out of the car, you stopped crying. It was the heat, it was the sunlight, I know it."

"It wasn't the heat," I tell her.

"The sunlight, you loved it."

"I didn't love it."

"Is that any way to speak to your mother?"

"I wouldn't know, would I?"

"I haven't been gone all that long."

"Since my sixth birthday," I say. "Nearly eight years."

"It feels like yesterday," she says. She sits up. Runs her fingers through my hair. "That long hair, always wild. Tangled. The same as when I left you."

"I look different."

"No," she says. "You don't."

Mom lies down flat, palms up, skin as pale as the outer light. She closes her eyes.

"Look under the bed," she says. "Another surprise."

I kneel against the floor, reach beneath the bed skirt. I pull out a paper hatbox. Inside, a blue sequined dress.

"How did you—?"

"Mothers know," she tells me without opening her eyes. "They always know."

I can't believe it, her coming back and her knowing.

"So you can go to the dance," she says.

I hold the dress in my hands and bury my face into the satin fabric.

"You're going to be beautiful," she tells me. "Everyone's going to love you."

I want to tuck myself beside her, lay my head against her chest, but I stay mad.

"Dad doesn't want me to go to the dance," I say.

I climb onto Dad's bed, far enough away so she can't touch me.

"We'll sleep now. We'll talk about the dance when your father gets back."

And it's just then that I realize he's gone, and I wonder where he is.

When Dad gets home, I'm sleeping on his bed. The orange blossom folded gently inside my hand.

Dad walks in the room. I can hear his boots drumming against the wood floor.

"Where were you?" I want to know.

I look up. Dad's covered in paint. Blue lines across his face.

"Did you see Mom?" I say. "She was just here."

"Go to bed," he tells me. "Your own bed."

The next morning, I wake up and watch the snow falling out the window.

On my nightstand, the orange blossom. A tar-colored mush.

"Mom," I call for her. "Where are you?"

I wander through the castle, up to the attic, to the new floor, calling her name, but she doesn't answer. In Dad's bedroom, the iron's out, still hot. I check the closets. Her floral suitcase is gone. I search the whole house, every cupboard. The blue dress is gone, and I think maybe Dad saw it and hid it because he doesn't want me to go to the dance. But it doesn't matter anymore. I'll get my own.

"A jacket," Dad says.

"Don't need one." I throw on Dad's boots. Rewrap the soles.

"Careful," he tells me. "The ice road. Be back before dark." And I know I've only got an hour to reach Onie.

I hurry out across the lake. Today, it's clear, too warm for a coat. Nearly thirty degrees. I can see the sea caves lining the island, empty now, iced over and waiting. I can see the peak of the lighthouse but not the castle. It's below the trees. Too small to see from this far out.

A Breakup Story, Catalogued in Guns
Jillian Merrifield

1) Gun number one was his brother's, a rifle from WWI, bought online and fired in their backyard. My boyfriend was home from school with mono. I was still in Rock Island crying in the hallway of my friend's dorm. She was watching American Idol and I was trying to explain why exactly I was so opposed to what he referred to as his civil rights.

2) Gun number two was his, a .22 caliber rifle. I was with him when he got it, standing awkwardly at the gun counter at Dicks as he signed the paperwork. I sat in the passenger seat of his Crown Vic on the way home and thought about getting pulled over. His mom didn't want to sign the FOID application at first. He made her.

3) Gun number three was a Mosin Nagant, just like his brother's. You could use them in Call of Duty. They were a one-hit kill if you shot somebody in the head. I liked them in the video game. He shot it in the backyard, scaring the livestock. I watched him clean it in his basement. I was spending more time at his house than I was supposed to, sixty miles from home in the west suburbs, a spin on the green line and the Metra. I always paid to get there.

4) I think the next gun was the pump-action shotgun. I'm pretty sure it was his favorite. We'd go buy ammo at the Farm and Fleet when we were in the north suburbs. He'd stock up and take it home with him on breaks. When we were out at school, we went to Wal Mart for ammo. I'd stand amidst the bullets and buckshot. I think he was happier to see the guns than his parents.

5) To be a cool girlfriend, I bought him a fancy scope for his birthday the second year we were together. He became obsessed with calibrating it. The only thing that rivaled his obsession for guns was comic books—Deadpool and Iron Man. He kept them in shoeboxes.

6) There were other weapons, other moments. He heard a noise in the night and brought a hatchet out to sit on the couch with us as we watched a movie at his parents' house. His mom came out of the bedroom to get a drink and didn't know why he had it out. I kept my eyes down because it was easier. I had taken him to Walmart to buy that hatchet after he had asked me to drive him there. Just because—no reason really. I took him in my roommate's CR-V. I didn't know that you could just buy a hatchet. No ID required.

7) I have a friend I've known for years. He lives in Missouri and has a concealed carry license. I went to hang out at his parents' place last summer—they

were out of town. He answered the door and just inside, on top of some books, was a revolver. He says if I don't want a gun but am afraid of people with guns, I should get a gun.

8) There was a time my boyfriend took me out to lunch, but it was really because there was a gun store nearby. By now, I'd been along to Dicks, Farm and Fleet, Walmart and Cabela's, but this was different. Numberless guns were on the walls and in the glass display, and behind the counter the man looked at me as much as he looked at my boyfriend.

9) The girls who lived in the apartment beneath mine were talking about getting a gun to defend themselves against the peeping Tom who kept visiting our triplex. The idea terrified me. The girls were always sloppy drunk, walking their naked orange bodies in front of the windows and having sex that echoed through the air ducts. It would be easy for them to misfire and hit our unit by accident. My roommate settled for pepper spray; she gave me a tire-thumper. By then, my boyfriend and I were broken up, but I had never even thought about the fact that he liked to get just as drunk as those sorority girls. He said he'd never bring a gun to school because he didn't trust his frat brothers when they were drunk. At least that's what he used to say. He'd gotten quiet on the subject towards the end.

10) The night he had me on his unmade bed in the smelly new frat house, it was December in Rock Island. I was telling him I didn't think we should give it another shot. He called me cruel and punched the walls. Nothing hung on them, but they rattled anyway like the drywall was just going to give up on the studs. I was thinking maybe I could make a break for my friend's house around the corner. I'd pound on the windows of his basement apartment and scare the shit out of him; he was probably playing video games in the dark. But I'd be followed. He said I was heartless, and it occurred to me that I should be scared of the weapons whose locations I no longer knew.

TRUST IN THE WILD
CHRIS HAVEN

I interrupted a robin pulling a worm out of the ground.
The bird dropped the worm, then did that little jitterbug
with its beak to the sky, head rocking back and forth
before swallowing it down. I walked by so close
the robin should have flown away but didn't. It wanted
that worm and I thought, what a resourceful robin.
That robin swallowed its fear for the meal. Of course,
the robin was lucky I wasn't a predator. I think,
maybe I've just given that robin a false sense of trust.
Maybe when there's a real threat, the robin will think,
I got this, nobody can touch me, I'm a robin, and then
the robin will get shot, or run over.
                              Before I was married,
I trained a random squirrel to take a nut from my hand.
It didn't take long. I wanted to impress my in-laws,
show them how patient I could be, how I could get wild
animals to trust me. *What a guy! Take our daughter!*
they would think. But they ended up more interested in
the squirrel than me. That squirrel is probably dead now.
I probably killed it, by instilling in it a false sense
of trust in the world. I wonder about that with other people,
my wife. My children. Whatever I give them, they will accept.
Whatever I have that I don't want taken will still be taken.
Whatever rules the world wants to make, it will make.

NEIGHBOR'S GARDEN
CHRIS HAVEN

The neighbor on the hill has a garden,
shiny gazing globes, wire fencing,
wooden slats building up the beds.
In the middle a tiny leafless tree hard as driftwood rises,
electric strike around a Tesla coil,
thought of a brain without the brain.
Maybe a man is buried below.
Above, pure idea.
It looked dead, no bud or bark.
One day I asked the man about the tree.
It was not native, dead a scant year after planting.
His wife said get rid of it, but he can't.
He's spray painted it pink.
Last year he'd done it in orange though it's hard to see
for the branching. It's a good garden but
he says this is what gets the most comments,
this dead thing in the center.

*   *   *

My son blows the trumpet, sometimes pure.
He doesn't know how he makes the sound.
Something like that tree, branching through his lungs.

*   *   *

We place ornaments on our fake tree.
A pickup with a throaty motor gurgles by.
I know the driver looks in our window.
It's a perfect picture as my children select the needles.
The driver will probably go hunting very soon
or maybe already has, carcass draped across the hood.
I can feel the hunter sorting his memories
as he looks in my window, not finding a match.
He longs for this scene that's unreal, even to me.

This longing puts gas in his truck,
the nick in the seed, the kind of longing
that none of us, even those of us who find it
at the dead center of our lives, can ever reach.

EVERY FAMILY HAS THAT ONE STORY THAT DRIVES SOMEONE TO STEAL

MARIANNA HOFER

Tiny birds settle in the lilac,
making a sound like that
of a slowly turning creek.
I clip basil with the clippers
inherited from an uncle dead
now for nearly 40 years.

After my uncle died, before
his sisters, my mother and aunt
sold their family home where
he and his wife, also now long
dead, had lived. My mother would
take me there with her to check
on the place, a massive farmhouse
alone on a slight rise out on Rt. 59,
five or six miles outside of Kent.

We'd walk to the back property line,
through the long run to ruin garden,
around the shambled chicken coop.
She might've told me a story from
her childhood, but mostly she fretted
over what would she and her sister do
with the place, or reran the tale of
one of the other older brothers who'd
thrown diplomas, birth certificates,
the family Bible, anything legal
or important, into the creek, then
shot himself. She'd look at me
as if I would one day do the same.

I was 19, so none of what she said
made much sense to me. I just walked,
often stopped listening to her, instead

listened to what seemed a constant
wind running through the tall weeds.

The property took a few years to sell.
But before then, between my uncle's
death and the sale, in the late Aprils,
my mother would drive us out there,
I'd get the clippers from the enclosed
back porch, and she'd have me cut
an armload or two of lilac branches,
fresh and bright smelling, from
a brittle rangy bush planted by her
mother at some point right next to
the back porch door, bark scaly,
mottled green-gray, yet determined
to bloom profusely each spring.

I have no idea why my mother came
to own those clippers—they seemed
such an odd piece to pick up among
the rest of what she brought home
after they no longer owned the place,
cleaned everything out—that sad last
box with some empty tins, a brass bowl,
wooden music box with a note "don't
wind tight" taped next to the key.

On some trip home, I nonchalantly
stole the clippers, slid them into
a back pocket, never mentioned
the theft to my mother. Here now
those tiny birds have gone simply
quiet in the darkening light.

BUT THEN THERE WAS THE DOG
RACHEL PROCTOR MAY

His car she sold. His clothes went in garbage bags to await their sentencing: basement or Goodwill. Out went his frozen burritos, his barbeque sauce, his slab of halibut from that trip to Alaska. His cheap shaving cream, his expensive shampoo, his fennel toothpaste. Gone. But the house was still full of him.

So she packed up all the photos they took together. The knick-knacks they bought together. Anything that had been a wedding present had to go, down to the mixing bowls and cutting boards. As the pile of unlabeled cardboard boxes grew in the basement, the house began to take on the flavorless, microwaved warmth of an extended-stay hotel.

But then there was the dog.

Penny had red hair, long legs, and a big mouth. She chewed, she jumped, she nipped when she got excited; she dug, she drooled, and she stank when she got wet. Jillian hated her. She had always hated her, from practically the second she had stepped out of her car and heard Nate yelling in the backyard.

"Come! Come! Penny, *come!*"

It was the tone of voice people use with dogs who will never, ever come.

Jillian had gone around the side of the house and joined Nate on the back porch. There was Penny, running in circles with a flailing gait halfway between windmill and squid. When she saw Jillian, she *did* come. She launched up the porch steps and leapt onto Jillian, her front paws reaching all the way to Jillian's shoulders. Jillian half-screamed, half-grunted as Penny's weight hit her.

"Whose dog?" she asked, pushing the paws off her shoulder. They were nearly as large as her hands.

"Ours," said Nate, grinning like Penny was an unexpected bouquet. "You like her? Look at that red hair!"

"She doesn't seem very trained. How old is she?"

"About two. And we can train her. She'll be an awesome dog. Look at those legs!" That was Nate: optimistic to the point of delusion.

"You can train her."

"You'll help, right? You're such a good dog person."

Jillian was a dog person, but she was not a bad-dog person. And Penny was a bad dog. For a year and a half, Nate had tried. The house was filled with training treats and squirt bottles and special disciplinary collars, but Penny had remained a stubborn red avalanche of slobber and jaws. And now that Nate was gone and wouldn't be out for eight years, Penny was hers.

*   *   *

The doorbell rang.

Jillian's biggest problem, other than Penny, was the house. She couldn't afford the payments on her own, but she didn't want to move. What she wanted was to magically wake up in a new house with empty closets and no holes in the walls where the pictures used to be. Instead, she was getting a roommate.

At the door was Molly, transformed from e-mail address to flesh. Molly had short black hair, a black tank-top, and looked to be in her late 20s. Both arms were thrashing oceans of koi and sea dragons, typhoons and bodhisattvas. She is a bass player and a chef, Cecile said when she told Jillian her friend's sister was looking for a place. She needed a roommate who wouldn't be bothered by her practicing, and who wouldn't let the bathroom get too disgusting. Apparently the two are inversely correlated. As for Jillian, all she really cared about was not having to explain anything.

"I'll e-mail her tonight," she had told Cecile. "Before I do, can you be sure to tell her about—you know?"

"Sure thing, hon," Cecile had said.

Jillian led Molly through the house—the living room, sparse as a savannah; the bathrooms, smelling of pine. Four bedrooms, purchased in anticipation of a future that now would never come.

Jillian had been dreading showing her house. She was not a chatty person to begin with, and now it seemed everything she said had to work its way out through a mouth full of Nate. "What are you doing this weekend?" friends would ask. "Nothing." *My husband went to jail.* She wasn't sure how she'd get through, saying the words "Here's the living room" without gagging on a*nd the furniture we bought when we moved in,* or "Here's my yoga room," *which was supposed to be the nursery for the first baby.* As it turned out, Jillian barely had to say a word. Molly filled the rooms with a resonant flow of commentary on paint colors, amplifier brands, and natural cleaning products, so all Jillian had to do was float along and remember to smile. It wasn't too hard. Molly made Jillian feel calm. Her whole demeanor suggested nothing could possibly be a big deal, and even if it were, she could handle it.

They ended up on the back porch. Jillian offered Molly sparkling water or beer, and Molly accepted a beer. Jillian pulled one from the six-pack that had been sitting next to the salad dressing forever, paused, and then took one for herself.

"I love it," said Molly, meaning the house. "Can I meet the dog? Cecile said you have one."

"Temporarily."

Penny was in her crate, which was in Jillian's room. When Jillian unlatched the crate, Penny burst out the door and scrambled down the stairs. She skidded across the kitchen tiles and into the back door, where she hopped onto her hind legs, her claws smacking the glass. Her tail thrashed like an angry cottonmouth that had gotten ahold of her hindquarters and had no intention of letting go. Jillian shoved her aside with a practiced thigh and turned the knob. Penny erupted through the door like a shopper in a Black Friday stampede. She slammed into Molly's chair on her way down to the stairs, spilling beer on Molly's hand. Molly slurped it off like someone used to being jostled while holding a beer.

"Wow," said Molly. "That's a hell of a dog. What is she?"

Penny began running in circles along the track she had beaten into the grass.

"Setter-lab, I think." she said. "Maybe some pit. She was my husband's. It's only until I figure out what to do with her." She picked up a tennis ball and threw it toward Penny, who had begun digging a hole by the fence. Penny dropped to her haunches and began jawing the ball as if it was sticky taffy. Her face took on a thoughtful expression as the mouth worked updownupdown, revealing occasional flashes of disintegrating neon felt.

"Why doesn't your ex take her?"

"Huh?" *Dammit, Cecile.*

"Cecile said you were getting a, um, messy divorce?"

"Sort of," said Jillian. Molly sat, Penny chewed, and Nate kicked Jillian in the roof of her mouth. "We're not divorced yet. He went to jail."

Molly widened her eyes and nodded slowly in an expression of tell-me-more sympathy, like a morning-TV hostess. Jillian realized she actually did want to tell her more.

"For screwing a high schooler."

Molly nodded some more. She didn't look at Jillian like she were roadkill, or the kind of wife who could drive her husband to jailbait. This is a big deal, her expression said, but we can handle it.

"What an asshole."

"He didn't know she was in high school."

"Oh, good. So he's an asshole, but not a perv."

Before she knew it was happening, Jillian laughed.

"And now you're stuck with the asshole's dog?"

"Temporarily."

Sip.

"I didn't know you could still go to jail for that," said Molly. "Aren't high schoolers screwing each other all the time? Hell, I was getting laid in the practice rooms after orchestra about every other week, and I'm at least a hundred and fifty years old."

"She got pregnant. And he paid for an abortion. And her daddy plays golf with the D.A."

"You're kidding. That's one unlucky asshole."

"And kind of pervish, I think. He's 36 and thought she was, like, 20."

"Yeah, kind of perv. Not Grade A, though. Minor league."

Penny spat out the remains of the ball and trotted to the porch. Jillian pulled another from the basket and threw it as far as she could.

Molly looked at her watch.

"So are we going to do this?" she asked.

"Let's do it."

"Good." Molly raised her bottle. "Here's to your asshole husband for finding me a place to live."

*   *   *

Molly moved in the next week. She practiced during the day when Jillian was at work, and was gone most nights at the restaurant or gigs or parties. She brought home leftovers, keeping the fridge full of tortilla soup and pumpkinseed enchiladas. The bathrooms sparkled like a beauty pageant ball gown. She even fostered a theatrically hearty hatred for Penny.

"Whoever named this dog was an idiot," she said, fighting to carry a cup of kibble to Penny's bowl as Penny leaped and nipped. "We should call her She-Devil."

"I'm taking care of it."

"Or Hellfire. Satan?"

Jillian suspected she didn't actually mind the dog that much, but as the weeks went on, Jillian felt that she should make good on her promise that the dog was only temporary. So she forced herself one Saturday afternoon to take Penny to the city shelter. She arrived and parked in the shade, where she sat for a minute. Then, leaving Penny's leash on the seat beside her, she rolled down the windows a crack, tossed an entire bag of rawhide treats into the backseat, and crossed the parking lot alone, hoping no one would recognize her. Before she met Nate, she had volunteered at the shelter for three years, taking dogs in the adoption program for a run a few days a week after work—exercise keeps them mellow, and mellow dogs find homes. Never in her life had she been in such good shape.

"Jillian!"

She should have known. Nobody ever quits at the city.

"Amy! Great to see you. How are things?"

Amy was at the intake desk, barely visible behind displays of brochures about responsible pet ownership.

"The same. Nuts as always."

"Busy?"

Amy rolled her eyes.

"You wouldn't believe it. Last Tuesday we took in *a hundred and fifteen dogs.* A hundred and fifteen dogs!"

"Horrible."

"And how are you? How's Nate?"

"Fine. What did you do with a hundred and fifteen dogs?"

The phone rang, and Amy kept talking as she reached for it.

"What do you think? We're full, all the rescues are full, the fosters are sick of us calling, and–oh, crap. Anyway, we miss you, hon. Good afternoon, Harristown Animal Shelter."

Jillian went back to the kennels. It was the same as ever–clanging chain link doors, alternating olfactory waves of feces and disinfectant, and the barking, an orchestra of pitch, timbre, volume, and tone. Some of the kennels were adorned with colorful "Adopt Me!" signs modeled after singles ads: "I like long walks on the beach. I just love to cuddle." And names: Bailey, Comet, Jasper, Cookie. Others sat in kennels identified only by number.

Jillian stopped before one of the numbered kennels. Inside was a black lab, laying on the ground with its chin in its paws. Jillian knelt, and the dog's eyebrows–such as they were–raised a little. She had gotten Cody here, her sweet black lab. Cody was a great dog. When he died, she paid the full $200 to get the deluxe cremation so the ashes she took home from the vet would be his alone.

She held the back of her hand up to the chain link and the dog leaned forward slightly to sniff it. It licked her skin gently, as if it were a rich dessert that came in very small portions.

"Excuse me."

A woman in scrubs was behind her, a vet tech with a leash in her hand. That meant one of two things: vaccinations and the adoption program, or sodium pentobarbital and the landfill. Jillian froze–not Black Lab!–but the woman just needed to get around her on the walkway. She entered a kennel a few doors down and after what sounded like a scuffle, came out dragging a powerful Dalmatian. His neck muscles strained against his leash and he barked a grating, hiccup-like bark as the tech hauled him across the lawn toward the medical wing. He'd be getting the blue juice, for sure.

She scratched Black Lab's nose. Jillian guessed he was about 6, which meant he'd probably get the blue juice, too. Turning kennels fast is how you keep dogs alive, and middle-aged dogs sit forever. The irony, Jillian had learned, is that most people don't actually know how to train a puppy, so the shelter was constantly sending home good puppies who came back a year later as bad dogs. No fault of their own, of course, but once they're damaged goods, they're damaged goods.

When Jillian got back to the car, Penny was most of the way through the bag of treats. Even with the windows down, she had gotten sweaty, and the car smelled sour. Jillian rolled the windows down all the way and drove home, her damaged-goods cargo chewing silently in the backseat.

*   *   *

The next week, Penny ate Molly's boots, the black lace-up ones she had brought home after a summer busking through Europe. For Jillian, it was automatic to keep anything leather or cloth or expensive or well, anything really behind closed doors. But Molly had been gigging late and kicked off her boots in the kitchen as she made a 3 a.m. omelet, and the next afternoon couldn't find them anywhere. It was only when Jillian found the rubber soles in Penny's crate that she figured out what happened.

The time had come.

"I'll do it this weekend," said Jillian. Molly hadn't asked, but she seemed relieved.

"Do you want me to do it? I kind of want to, now." She looked at Penny. "Payback's a bitch, bitch."

"I can do it."

That afternoon, she took Penny on an extra-long run. It was October, and finally starting to get cool. Autumn used to be her favorite season, but it was also the month when Nate had been charged, so this year it felt like he had taken October from her, along with the rest of the year and everything else. Spring was when he went away, after the D.A. pulled out a stack of text messages and he changed his plea. Summer was the worst. That's when they had been screwing after community theater rehearsals of *A Chorus Line*. Jillian tried not to think about it, but every time she drove by the theater, she wondered where and how–the sound booth? The prop closet? Smack in the middle of the stage under a single spotlight? So now her commute was 10 minutes longer, and her only unencumbered season was winter.

She hung Penny's leash by the door and picked up the mail. The packet from DIYdivorce.com had come. If she started now, and if Nate didn't make a fuss, they would be done by December. Another unwanted anniversary. Better to wait.

The mail also contained brochures for ski resorts. They came every day. In what proved to be one of his last major purchases as a free man, Nate had booked a trip to Colorado last winter, which he hadn't told Jillian about. At first it was presumably going to be a surprise, and then later they weren't speaking except through lawyers. Jillian found out when the charges for the deposit showed up on the credit card bill. She only thought it was for the high schooler for a second–not even Nate was that delusional–but she called anyway and yes, the reservations named her and Nate. Goddamn. She had always wanted to go to Colorado.

"That's what was so weird about it," she told Molly. "Everything was great, I thought. But people don't just screw around for no reason."

"The hell they don't," Molly had said. "Some guys like dessert, no matter how much prime rib they're getting at home. Nate was an idiot, an asshole, and probably blind and mentally retarded, too."

Jillian nodded. Molly had never met Nate. She thought he was just a small, stiff thing you could fold up and fit into a box. Contents: One Asshole. To Jillian he was intangible and everywhere; a liquid, a particle, a wave. He was a discrete tattoo, something tangled in her hair. He took up half her bed at night, and only snuck away when she opened her eyes. Molly held out a box and told Jillian to just pack him away, like she had packed up his guitar and his socks. Jillian filled her box with words, but the more she talked, the more she realized it was the anger she wanted gone, not him, not really. But he was gone, and so was her life, and so he was an asshole. Someday, Jillian hoped, he'd stop spilling out of the box. But she also wondered what would be left of her when he did.

*   *   *

Friday morning, she did it. She went to the shelter with Penny, and drove to work in a car reeking with guilt. Jillian wondered if knowing that Penny would almost certainly get blue-juiced made her more culpable than people who kept themselves ignorant about what would happen to their pets. She pictured Penny in a kennel, pawing at the door and whining. This isn't my fault, she told herself. I'm not the one who got myself sent to prison. I'm not the one who brought a bad dog home in the first damn place.

"Feel better?" asked Molly when Jillian came home.

"No."

"You should," said Molly. She was making herself a sandwich and, without asking, started making Jillian one too. "You never wanted that dog and you shouldn't be stuck with her."

"Yeah."

"You're still coming tomorrow, right?" Molly had invited her to one of her parties. Music people. Jillian hadn't wanted to go. Music people hang with theater people and all the theater people know. But Molly had been relentless: "You're not the one who got locked up," she had said. "Don't live like you are."

Now, as she stood at the stove, grilling ham and gruyere in somebody's boxers and knee socks, Molly launched into a reprise. "Out with the old and in with the new, baby. You ditched the devil dog; now it's time to get yourself laid." She slid a spatula under a sizzling sandwich and flipped it onto a plate.

Jillian took the plate from Molly. If Penny had been there, she would have been pawing at her leg, hoping Jillian would get frustrated enough to drop her some ham. But Penny was gone.

The party was at Molly's drummer's house, a poorly maintained bungalow where everything was either lovingly curated or on the verge of collapse. Into the latter category fell the smelly, stained couch, the jelly jar glasses, and the entire bathroom. The former included a variety of vintage lamps and a Rock-Ola jukebox that played real 45s. Molly moved through the crowd comfortably, greeting nearly everyone. Jillian saw a couple guys she knew and quickly turned away.

"Where can I get a drink?"

"Back porch, probably. Bobby usually keeps a cooler out there."

The backyard was lit by Christmas lights, tiki torches, and a firepit. The crowd around the cooler was thick, so Molly left Jillian on a porch swing and squeezed her way in. It was the kind of party she and Nate would have gone to a decade ago, before their friends started buying real glasses and going to bed by 11. It felt both familiar and wrong, like finding a once-favorite outfit in the back of your closet and realizing it's out of style and no longer fits.

"Jill!" Molly had come back with two beers and a tall man. "I want you to meet my friend Matt. Matt's an environmental lawyer and plays guitar. What's your band again, honey?"

"Unimpeachable."

"You're kidding. You're not kidding. That's way too cute."

"Sorry you disapprove, Mol."

"Don't worry, I disapprove of everything. Except Jillian. She's my roomie. Jillian's a landscape architect. And a painter."

"What do you paint?" asked Matt.

"I did a lot of set design," said Jillian, peeling at the label of her beer. Not even two minutes and she was talking about theater. "Backdrops and things. I've been too busy with work lately, though. So where does Unimpeachable play?"

"Jill! Matt!" Molly was dragging two more guys over. "Do you guys know Forest and Jordan?"

Things continued like this for a while, with Molly bringing over people she introduced with a name and something other than a day job. The faces and conversation topics came and went; bands, beers, food trucks, film festivals, adventure races. Jillian learned the word "parkour." Everyone seemed so young. Eventually, Jillian found herself alone on the swing with Matt.

"So what kind of environmental lawyer are you? The tree-huggy kind or the keep-the-lights-on kind?"

"Ha. You know your lawyers. Most people just assume I'm the tree-huggy kind." He pushed the swing back and forth with a scuffed suede boot.

"The people who hire me hire a lot of lawyers. Mostly to get them out of hugging any more trees than they have to."

"I'm the whoever-pays-me kind. I do permitting, mostly."

"How'd you get into that?"

"Hugging trees," he said. "How about you?"

"The same, I guess. I like plants. I wanted to do something visual but also get a paycheck. So how long have you been playing with Unimpeachable?" Jillian would rather talk about him than her.

"Couple years. We started playing in law school."

Jillian realized he was younger than he looked. "Have you recorded?"

Matt laughed. "We barely even play out. Molly just has that thing where she hates to define people by their jobs. And so," he said, putting an arm around the back of the swing, "tell me about your job."

They talked about water features and green roofs and clients from hell. Matt got up twice to get them fresh beer. Jillian barely ever drank anymore, and quickly got tipsy. There was a lot of laughing. Somehow, they got talking about music they liked when they were kids. Jillian: Whitney Houston and Madonna. Matt: Bel Biv DeVoe and the Backstreet Boys. Then came movies, then TV shows. Jillian thought he was a pop culture freak. Then, as he Wikipediaed *The Wonder Years* to find out when it had run, she finally got it: he was trying to figure out how old she was. Suddenly, her head was no longer filled with a fuzzy cloud, but with a swarm of pissed-off bees. She felt heavy.

"Another beer?" she asked, standing.

She texted Molly while she was at the cooler, and came back with a beer for him and a Coke for herself. "I told Molly I'd drive," she said. "I'm the responsible old lady in the house."

Matt laughed. "Molly needs an old lady."

"You'd be surprised. You should see her clean the bathroom."

Ten minutes later, Molly appeared. "Hey, kids."

"Hey, Mom," said Jillian. "Speak of the devil."

"You want to see the devil? That'll be me during the breakfast rush if I don't get to bed before one."

"That's cool," said Jillian. She turned to Matt. "Nice to meet you."

"You, too."

"Maybe I'll see you around."

"Let me know if you need to sue a tree."

"Let me know if Unimpeachable is playing."

They social-hugged but didn't exchange numbers.

*   *   *

"I'd like to get my dog back."

It was the next morning. Jillian, hung over, was at the shelter. She had meant to arrive when it opened, but she had overslept and it was almost noon.

"How do you know she's here?"

"I dropped her off Friday morning. Owner-surrenders get 48 hours, right?"

"If they don't make it into the adoption program." The intake woman typed Jillian's information into the computer. "Kennel 133."

Walking through the shelter, Jillian asked herself what she was doing. She didn't want Penny. She had promised Molly that Penny would go. But waking up in her empty house, she realized she wanted Penny gone even less than she wanted Penny around. Plus, it wasn't Penny's fault that she was damaged goods. She should try harder, find some rescue group, find a no-kill shelter in another city. Or hell, maybe try to train her. She had left that to Nate; she had never really tried. Penny was almost four, maybe her puppy energy would finally start to mellow out.

Kennel 133 was empty. Jillian returned to the front desk.

"133?" She asked.

"That's right."

"I checked 133. It's empty."

"Maybe someone typed it in wrong. Did you check the rest of the kennels?"

Jillian walked along all the runs. No Penny.

"Did she get dispo'ed?" she asked when she returned. "It should be in the computer. Or maybe someone took her home? A rescue group?"

"Do you want to look? It says she's in 133 and that no, she hasn't had her disposition assessment yet. Or been rescued." She typed some more. "Oh," she said, frowning.

"What?"

"It just refreshed."

"And?"

"She got dispo'ed. Not suitable for the adoption program."

"So where is she?"

"Well," the woman paused. "You know the techs usually start on the list in the afternoon."

For the third time, she returned to the runs. 133 was still empty; Penny was still nowhere. When she went back to intake, the woman was helping someone else. From time to time, she glanced at Jillian.

"She's definitely, definitely not there," Jillian said when it was her turn.

"All I know is what's in the computer."

"Can you call the vet techs?"

The woman gave her a hard look. "Do you really want me to?"

No, she didn't. Yes, she did.

"Could you?"

The woman picked up the phone and dialed. "Hey guys. There was an owner-surrender in 133. Wondering if you've seen it. It was on your list." She paused and listened.

"Yeah. 133. Lab mix. Red. Yeah. Oh. Right. Okay."

Jillian watched the woman, whose eyes were cast down at a pen she was using to draw stars and hearts on a pad by her phone.

"Never mind. Thanks," Jillian said when the woman hung up.

"Sorry."

"It's not your fault."

Jillian sat in the lobby for a minute, then went back into the kennels. Dogs barked, chain link clanged, fluorescent lights reflected on the wet floors where recently emptied kennels had been hosed down. The floor of kennel 133 was slick and shiny, ready for its next occupant. Jillian walked slowly along the runs. Maybe she should start volunteering again. Or maybe she should take home a dog. A nice, mellow, middle-aged dog. One who was sweet but bland, maybe even a little ugly. She knelt before a few kennels but none seemed right, not even the half-dozen nameless black labs.

She drove home alone, with the windows rolled up. The car didn't smell like Penny. It smelled like nothing at all.

ONE SWING
MATT HURLEY

Stepping into the batter's box, Luke tapped his bat on home plate and studied the old son of a bitch on the mound. Detective Frank "Elbows" Marconi dug a cleat into the dirt and offered a sneer in return. It was no secret they hated each other. Luke went deep twice against Elbows at the start of the season, propelling the Kane County Courthouse Challengers to their first-ever victory over the East Kenwood Combined Policemen and Firemen's Badgers. Elbows was the reason Luke hadn't seen his daughter since.

The Kane County Courthouse Challengers were down 6-5 with two outs in the bottom of the seventh and final inning. Jamie Parker stood on second base in tight yoga pants and a t-shirt cut at her midriff, doing her best to distract the shortstop. Luke could end it with one swing and send them to the playoffs for the first time since he'd joined the team.

Elbows' tall, lanky frame looked like a marionette being pulled in all directions as he kicked one leg up, pulled his arm back, and let loose with a spinning pitch that curved in on Luke as it crossed the plate.

"Strike one!" called the umpire, thrusting his hand out in dramatic fashion and raising the tension on both benches. Luke thought the pitch was inside, but kept quiet. Cries of "bullshit!" came from his teammates behind him, and Luke was pleased to know they were still invested in the game. Two cases of empty beer cans littered their dugout and more drinks waited at Tupper's Bar & Grill. But it seemed they craved a win as much as he did. The catcher tossed the ball back to the mound and mumbled, "tough pitch."

Their win in May was cause for celebration, just like every other game, win or lose. Luke knew he should have walked home at the end of the night. He blamed himself when an off-duty Detective Marconi pulled him over two blocks from his house, on a seldom-patrolled road. After blowing a .09, he accepted the rough treatment—face shoved into the hood of his car, nightstick poking his kidneys, handcuffs too tight—and went quietly, jaw clenched in anger. Luke would never forget the look Marconi gave him as he closed the door of the mattress-less cell that stank of urine and left Luke behind.

When his ex-wife, Stacey, bailed him out the next morning with Amelia in tow, he felt lower than he ever had. She followed up the arrest with a visit to family court a few weeks later. He lost visitation rights and could do nothing but watch and curse Elbows Marconi as Amelia broke out in tears across the courtroom and screamed for her daddy.

Luke missed his little girl—the way she curled up in his lap when he read to her, and the way she giggled when he made goofy faces. He wanted to sign her up for softball in the spring, and he longed to teach her how to swing a bat, how to catch a fly, and how to get her glove down in front of grounders. He wanted to coach her team and buy them all pizza and ice cream no matter the outcome. Stacey, despite her love of all things baseball, was not good at sports herself, and didn't want Amelia playing, either. Without him around, Luke feared she might sign her up for the Little Miss Kenwood Cheerleading Squad.

Elbows stood upright on the mound, twisting the ball in his glove to find the right grip. His face was drawn and his eyes were tired. A patchwork of wrinkles made him seem older than his fifty-five years. He'd be retired if it weren't for the Badgers. They were three-time league champions and Elbows had won all but two of the victories during that stretch.

Luke knew a long ball down the line could end it. The left fielder was a heavy-set guy named Fitz who was surprisingly quick. But put it over his head and Luke would be rounding third and chasing Jamie Parker home before Fitz even got a glove on it. Elbows did his awkward windup and let the ball fly, starting outside and moving in as it neared the plate. Luke took a swing at it, but too early. The ball went high and deep but was clearly foul, crashing through a collection of elm trees before bouncing off the brick wall of the Kincaid Park Gymnasium.

"Strike two!" the umpire bellowed, as though anyone needed to be told. Luke stepped out of the box, set the bat between his legs, and brushed his hands on his baseball pants. He looked at his teammates, who leaned on the dugout fence. The sun fading into the trees behind right field still cast a warm glow onto the players, and boozy sweat poured from their brows. They were all decked out in colorful shorts or sweats, except Dave Halsey, who seemed uncomfortable in a worn pair of jeans.

In the field, the Badgers stood soldier-like and evenly spaced across the grass. They wore matching gray pants, gold jerseys, and hats with silver badges stitched on with the letters EKCPFB in bold type. The heat seemed to have no effect on them.

Despite the beer, the Challengers were playing like a team that belonged in the playoffs, and one that might have the Badgers' number once more. Grounders that generally skipped out of the infield were snagged and thrown for outs. Line drives were picked out of midair. They even turned a rare double play to the shock of everyone, including the umpire, who almost called the runner safe. Their offense clicked as well, at least for one inning. They scored all five of their runs in the fifth, on a rare bad inning for Elbows. It started with a walk to Jamie Parker— wiggling her hips and smiling without taking the bat off her shoulder—and ended with a three-run home run by Steve Sweeney.

As he stepped back into the batter's box, a cry of "Come on Luuuuuuuuuuuke!" sounded out. Phil, a thirty-something clerk who caught most games, showed some rare enthusiasm and the rest of the team chimed in with cheers. It made him hungry for the win. The disdainful smile on Elbows' face reminded him of the night of his arrest, and he wanted more than anything to wipe it clean. He still feared retribution, he knew what Elbows and the rest of the force were capable of. But what more could they do? He'd already lost his daughter, and she was all that mattered.

Luke sized up Elbows as he went into his windup. He could tell Elbows thought he already had him beat, and that made him even hungrier. Beneath the mocking look, Luke saw the lined face of a man who never progressed through the ranks of the police force. He'd heard rumors that his wife had left him earlier that year. Under different circumstances, Luke might feel sorry for him. But Elbows knew about Amelia, even threw out a "How's the kid?" comment when they crossed paths during pregame warm-ups. As he drew the ball back, Luke expected something out of the strike zone. He fought off the urge to swing and laid off as the ball dropped harmlessly onto the plate and bounced into the catcher's mitt. The umpire, if he was tempted to call a strike so he could go home, had no choice but to let it go.

Luke had been a star shortstop on the North Kenwood High baseball team for three years, and pro and college scouts would come watch him play. When he was drafted in the twenty-third round of the First-Year Player Draft by the Cubs, Stacey, then his high school sweetheart, convinced him he was big league material, and he skipped school to join the minors. But after three years, he was still stuck in Single A ball, and when Amelia was born that fall, he knew he needed to quit the game he loved.

When he took a job as a bailiff at the Kane County Courthouse, they gave him a spot on the softball team. He brought Amelia to every game until Stacey found out he was taking her to Tupper's for post-game celebrations. She accused him of cheating and kicked him out when she showed up at the bar and caught Jamie Parker massaging his shoulders. Luke knew Stacey wanted to be the wife of a ballplayer, and she resented him for not making it. It would never work out, no matter what he did.

The next pitch came in as hard as Elbows could throw it. Luke took a step forward, lifted the bat off his shoulder and stopped just short of swinging. It was outside, he knew, but barely, and with the way the umpire had been calling it, he took a deep breath and waited.

"Ball two," said the umpire, matter-of-factly. There were groans from the opposing bench and Elbows looked in and raised his hands in disgust.

"It was outside," the umpire yelled back. Then, just to Luke, "Not by much. This game better end on you swinging."

Luke stepped out of the batter's box while the umpire cleared home plate with his brush. He thought maybe it would be better if it didn't end on him swinging. The umpire would call strike three, Luke would argue briefly and that would be that. Elbows would take his team into the playoffs and stay off Luke's back. The season would be over for him and he could focus on seeing Amelia again. He wanted to take her hiking up Bald Mountain in the cool fall weather, or apple picking at Devoe's if she wanted. And he would spoil her with presents at Christmastime if he could only get visitation rights back. But he couldn't erase the memory of the night Marconi pulled him over, the look that said, "I own you."

Elbows twisted the ball in his palm again and Luke knew it was his pitch. Elbows was trying to outsmart him, coax Luke into a harmless pop-up, or maybe a routine ground ball to the shortstop for the final out. When it came across the plate, it stayed in just a little more than Elbows had intended, right where Luke wanted it. He could still feel Marconi's hot, stinking breath on his neck. He tightened his grip and swung with vengeance.

The ball came screaming off the bat like a shot. It went straight at Elbow's head and he had no time to react. He went down, his puppet strings snipped, and lay lifelessly on the mound. The ball continued on its trajectory and bounced toward second base.

Luke watched, never stepping from the batter's box as the shortstop picked the ball up on one hop, took two steps, and fired to first. Dave Halsey was retching over the dugout fence and a soft breeze pushed the smell of bile mixed with fresh-cut grass across the field. Luke didn't even bother running to first. The game was over.

After calling Luke out, the umpire hurried to the mound to check on Elbows. The East Kenwood Combined Policemen and Firemen's Badgers all rushed in from the field. Luke took a couple of steps toward the mound, trying to process what happened. He peered through the bodies and saw Elbows lying in a heap, arms and legs twisted. Fitz was kneeling on the ground next to him, saying his name and shaking him gently. Someone else pushed his way through with a first aid kit and knelt down next to Fitz.

Behind him, in the dugout, someone was on the phone.

"Kincaid Park Softball Field. We need an ambulance. There's been an accident."

Luke stepped closer. He could see the welt sprouting at the side of Elbows' head, and wondered if he were breathing. Then a hand was in his chest and another gripped his shoulder. The catcher was facing him, blocking him from the mound.

"What do you think you're doing?" he asked. "Planning to finish the job?"

Others who had been attending to Elbows stood up and moved closer to Luke. Luke eyed them with confusion and then looked down at his own hand. He was still holding his bat. He should have dropped it then, he knew. Put his hands up and backed away. Instead, his grip tightened as several Badgers inched toward him. He heard angry shouts from his own teammates, who were all watching from just outside the dugout. They scrambled onto the field, Steve Sweeney leading the pack, and rushed to his aid.

He never raised the bat, never took a swing. The sun had dipped behind the trees and the darkened faces created a more sinister mood around the infield.

Someone grabbed him from behind and pushed his arms behind his back. The bat fell and bounced with a tinny ring that echoed around the field. He was wrestled to the ground, face pressed into the grass with a heavy forearm.

Dust collected around him as he was surrounded by a crush of bodies moving above him. He tried to pull himself up, but a knee in the back denied his attempt. He spotted a pair of gray baseball pants and reached up, grabbing a handful of gold jersey and tried to yank it down. A gloved hand swung at his head, stinging his cheek, and he released his grasp. Arms and legs flailed around him as punches were thrown and bodies shoved in all directions. He caught a spiked cleat in the ribs and curled up to protect himself, unsure where the kicks were coming from. He swung his arms around wildly, trying to keep stray feet away from him.

Looking up, he saw Elbows still laid out on the mound, untouched by the melee around him. He wondered if Elbows had a daughter of his own, a few years older than Amelia, someone he hadn't seen in a long time. He pictured Amelia in her favorite Scooby Doo pajamas, ached to tuck her in and brush hair out of her face and kiss her on the forehead once more, just as a heavy foot connected with his head and everything turned to black.

No Short Way Out
NICK OSTDICK

FIRST APPEARED IN *NIGHT TRAIN*

What she told me before I left, was that I have until sunup.

Some strange curfew, straight outta left field.

She said, I'm not kidding, Danny, lips drawn tightly together. I didn't have to see it. I knew the sound of Quinn's clenched mouth in the darkness of our bedroom, walls untouched by light or shadow.

It's not even my fault. It's Blink's fault because his wife Dolly finally left him tonight and we're out on his boat over Lake Bracken, just drifting with the motor off and interstate-sounds rushing through the trees. Blink doubles up on the Old Style, knocking them back one after the other and then works a worm onto a hook.

You gonna drop a line or what? he asks.

I tell him I haven't been fishing much lately, that it's kind of left me, but he shakes his head at me and so I just bait one for the hell of it and drop one down.

Me and Blink are boys, real tight, and have been since our daddies worked nightshift at the gum factory. We know the pinch of cold winter earth through holes in the bottoms of our shoes. I can read the slightest flicker in his voice. He always finds which coals of mine to stoke.

I lean the pole against the inside of the boat so he won't notice, and I ask him if he caught the Sox score, and he lowers his head for a moment and says, No, I guess I must have missed it with my wife leaving me and all, you dumbshit, his left eyelid fluttering about a hundred miles an hour.

It's always like that, Blink's left eye, flapping away as if there's something caught in it. It gets worse when he's nervous or pissy. When he's drinking or when we're smoking a little or just before he's ready to haul himself out behind The Halfway to duke it out with a couple of wise asses who've given him a hard time. Sparks eating up a fuse, that's what he's always like, and he uses his eye as an excuse for all the bad shit in his life.

Sometimes it's funny, like at The Halfway when the cook burns his double bacon burger—That guys's got a prejudice against handicapped people, man, Blink says, mushing buns in his hands.

Other times though, like tonight, it's less funny, when he bursts a can of beer with his pocket knife and holds it above his head and lets the foamy mess fall into him and tells me the reason Dolly is leaving is because she can't take it anymore: the way his eye dances around in its socket and oozes like rotten vegetables.

She can't handle it, he says. Once in a while I'll ask her to help me put those drops in, and you'd think I was asking to fuck her ass with all the fuss she makes.

Maybe it's all a mistake, I say. Maybe she'll be back.

Yeah, maybe someday I'll see in 20/20, Blink says.

He oars the boat along because the engine will scare off any potential catch. We must be nearing the sandbar on the other side of the lake because the pines smell strong. The dark turns the shoreline purple and fuzzy and I don't know how the hell he spots it, but Blink stops rowing and wobbles to his feet and says, There, right there, voice pitching up.

I tell him I can't see a thing, and he oars us forward, maybe twenty or thirty more feet until I see it just beyond the stern: a half-submerged stump, branches sticking in the air like a massive spiderweb, and this brassy looking waterhole between the stump and the shore with a tiny opening of water that looks almost like it's swirling around, as if being drained from below.

Blink stows the oar. He grunts like it weighs a thousand pounds. He lights a cigarette and swoops his long goose-grey hair back on his head, embers trailing the path of his hand.

Would take the perfect cast, Blink says, flicking his line out. The cast holds in the air for a moment and then drops right into that water hole, his words like prophecy.

Your turn, he says.

I'll just watch for a bit, I say.

What the hell for?

I just don't feel like it, alright?

Then why we even out here? I can fish by myself anytime. Ain't no fun if we ain't competing.

I pop a beer, don't bother grabbing one for him. He watches me pull the tab free and toss it over the side, and then something snags and his reel spins wild, the sound of his line unwinding like a hive-worth of bees lowering onto us. It takes Blink a moment to snap into it, propping his cigarette in the corner of his mouth.

Get it, I holler.

Shut up, he replies, rod bending so hard it almost double-backs.

Water slaps against the boat. I tell him it must be a real hoss, and Blink wheezes in laughter and says, Like Dolly, spitting the cigarette from his mouth and puffing his cheeks as if trying to impersonate her. It makes no sense to call her fat. Dolly's a looker, real soft, powdery skin and eyes so blue they stick like a knife.

Like Quinn, actually, they could be twins they look so much alike. Almost like they split a brain too, and she always hassles me 'bout not speaking my mind or ever really challenging Blink or whatever. Like when her and I are splitting a bottle of bourbon on the front porch and watching the neighborhood kids drag their sparklers across the night, she'll say, You always defend him, you know that? Nobody can say anything bad about him.

I don't dog your friends, I say.

She smiles. A sly, peek-a-boo-I-can-see you kind of thing. Friend? she says.

It's like you're the same godblessit person.

Don't know about that. I'm far better to you than he is to Dolly.

Neither one of you is going to win Husband of the Year.

We ain't married, darling, I say, and she doesn't say anything else and doesn't bother to give back the bottle.

OK, Blink might be a little tough on the edges, but I wish she could've seen him earlier when he came by the house to get me. I wish she could've seen him sitting there in the dusty glow of his truck, sticking his palm with a fish hook, little spots of blood growing in his skin.

She's gone, Blink said. She's really gone and you gotta come with me. You gotta.

I wish Quinn could've seen his face, plowed up by loneliness and anger. She wouldn't have been able to say no. Look at his bloody palm. She'd understand. No man is a one hundred percent good guy all the time.

Get the fucking net, Blink says now, leaning back on his haunches, readying for one final pull. Hold it over the edge. I'm gonna drop it right in.

The water is cool and damp and I can taste the scum and I lean over the edge of the boat. The fight continues for another moment. Blink cranks on his reel, lets the pull of the fish drag him forward. Then he jerks back hard and there's this snap like someone's broken a branch over their knee and it's his line splitting in two, the hook and worm backfiring and catching Blink right in the face, the hook nesting into his hair and the worm dangling from his ear.

He looks insulted. The corners of his mouth sag and droop. Everything seems still, even his hinky eye, stuck wide open now. The fish is gone, jumps once or twice in the darkness, and Blink tosses the worm into the water and slowly untangles the hook from his hair. He picks up his rod to check it, bending it, testing it.

For a moment, Blink looks small and broken, like we're back in the cab of his truck and he's sticking himself with a hook. But then he runs a hand down the side of his face, scratches the stubble, and with this sneaky, sad grin says, Doesn't that goddamn fish know who we are?

He leans over the side of the boat.

Hey you son of a bitch, do you know who I am?

I laugh. Tell him, I say. Don't make us come in there after you, hands funneled at the sides of my mouth.

But Blink's not laughing now. He's just staring at the water, bent at the knees, frozen solid. After another moment, he lets the rod fall. He pulls his arms close to his sides. He sucks a breath and then tumbles forward into the water and disappears down, diving.

I stop laughing. I can't see him. I rub my eyes. I call out. But nothing finds me except owls off in the distance and a wind through the pines.

Can Blink swim? I don't know, I don't know if he can swim or not, I've never seen him do it. I can swim, but I don't know about Blink and I feel like I should and then he finally pops to the surface a few feet away, floating just fine but winded.

What the hell are you doing? I say.

He spits water. He pulls his hair out of his eyes. Help me, Danny. C'mon, help me get that thing. We can't let her get away. We can't.

Her? I say. But it's too late. He takes another deep breath and slips out of sight.

I quickly shuffle to the back of the boat to start the motor and give chase, but when I reach to yank the ripcord, my fishing pole rattles around the front and slips from its lean onto the floor. Ten minutes ago it would've been gone in the darkness, but now I can sorta see it there, baited, and I can smell the lake, that sour, shit-and-piss smell that sticks and soaks your skin. It's heavy. It's unmistakable. It's the sound of Blink calling out for me to follow him in. It's the echoes of Quinn's voice as she warns not to walk out the door. It's the pinch in my chest that cripples me as the dawn starts showing golden and pink in the water below—all this goddamn water and no short way out.

GATHERING OF CRANES
JAMES BARNETT

I have been to the Platte River
where the sandhills gather each spring
by the tens of thousands.
I have sat in the blind
face level with the mud
and listened
as the dawning sun
broke wide
the grey monochrome,
awoke a thousand voices,
primeval,
called forward
from an earlier age.
And then they fly
scattered
here and there
then all at once,
their awkward bodies
ill-designed for takeoff,
but up they go nonetheless
calling to one another
with throaty squarks,
they circle,
regather,
then escape
their muddy camp
leaving us in the blind
to greet the return of country quiet
alone.

They are also here,
at home,
off the Salt Creek
or the DuPage,

high above,
gathering for that last push
into the north woods,
their calls echoing off the ranch homes,
the Tudors, the Cape Cods,
sharing the day
with the emergent crocus
and tulip.

LAST HURRAH
JAMES BARNETT

Swimming off the Warren Dunes,
watching a storm
come across the lake
on the last day of summer.

The water is still
almost warm
on this September day.

Clouds break up the sun;
the rays falling like rain
sink in to the lake
to the west.

I float in deep water.
Dive down.
A dull lime green,
the shade of a polished desert rock,
the freshwater sea surrounds me.
Surfacing,
I see the sky darken.
Time to swim back
to shore.

RURAL LEGEND
JESSIE JANESHEK

I'll leave this place
of motors, rust wristlets
once autumn comes on
and night cats eat the poultice
the lumberjack spread
to jaundice my heat.

The weight of your panic
is the way to my nurture
yet you say it's different
when we drink on the slagheap
preacherman lingers
and your infant son wishes
his legs away.

I knit shut my teeth
when it's all intake
dead batteries, cigarettes.
The stench of repairmen
is the stench of short days
cotton ball angels, mesh wings
and candlelight stretched,
the wallpaper print in the attic
a mad kitten toile.

Lace oozes from eggs.
You tell me that grandpa
batted in twenty runs
left us death's secret.
It smelled just like whiskey.

THE INSTALLATIONISTS
TODD MERCER

It's the night before ArtPrize opens, and we're making love on a stack of old towels in a hollow space inside a huge installation that looks like a rambling. ship-wrecked house.

The old me didn't use terms like "making love," but Astrid turned me around this week. Everyone needs to re-think what's reflexive, because the lazy thought produces junk, she tells me. Re-purpose terms mindfully for maximum meaning. So I hardly ever say "fuck" anymore.

Astrid and I rolled into Grand Rapids before tons of component materials arrived in wooden crates. We worked nine days building The House-Ship. Prying with crowbars, unwrapping kitchenwares, slow work to be doing carefully. Astrid broke down crates and stuffed bits between soft goods on the port side.

I don't know how Astrid decided when the work was complete , but she placed one more vintage paperweight and said, "There." I could see she was right to stop.

A busted player piano, stacks of tattered leather-spined books, vinyl records, fabric samples, a montage of Depression glass. Bed spring and sofa skeleton. Window shutters with partly delaminated slats, the cross-section of contrasting paint layers—a modern archeology of someone's indecision in domestic design. We built a linen closet from bedstead spindles in the starboard wall, and jammed it with towels. The last few wouldn't compact enough to keep from hanging out. We constructed little rooms inside the House-Ship's hull, left gaps for patrons to peek at what Astrid's saving for those who were the most curious.

"Can you come help me? Do you have that much time?" Astrid had asked.

Could, and for once, did. So I went. We were only friends. I wanted to watch her creative process from a front-row seat. My assets were endless patience and willingness to eat fast food while stacking disconnected chair-backs, and spreading small-chunk concrete rubble as inland beach sand.

I believed in her vision.

Now we're sweating, adding each other to our life-lists in an interior section reserved for Ball jars and Japanese lanterns, candelabra as porthole bars.

Men get lonely too; I'd be lying if I said I wasn't thrilled not to be alone.

*   *   *

Astrid and I accidentally sleep through the night. We wake to the voices of art voyeurs, ("Oh my God, look what they did here!") taking perspective on the overall effect from the bow, the edge of the indoor beach-head.

They'll walk circles around it and see what we've constructed to tell a story.

As Astrid stirs, they'll see light shining out the cracks. Follow the light, they'll see us tucked under a canvas sail, Astrid's head full of ideas raising and lowering, her starboard cheek floating on my chest-bellows.

We won't be dressed when people start trooping through. Astrid didn't mean for us to become part of the exhibit, but I haven't felt this innocent in a hell of a long time.

WELCOME TO MILWAUKEE
SAM SLAUGHTER

Dave told me he needed help on a project, and I was the only one he trusted. He said there would be pizza, but asked me to bring beer. I agreed.

"Don't tell me this is some sort of murder-suicide thing," I had joked. He didn't laugh.

"Just get over here," he said.

On the way to his house, I stopped and grabbed a case of High Life. The door was unlocked when I got there and a sticky note told me to meet him upstairs. Dave still lived in his parents' house—in the basement—and we used to spend a good amount of our time there stoned, staring at the feet that passed by on the sidewalk outside the basement window. When we were teens, we played this game where we guessed the person's entire life story just by their shoes. Dave was always better at it. The game had continued through college, happening less and less until finally, when I got my job, it stopped completely. I avoided the basement as much as I could, and Dave never brought it up.

Somewhere upstairs, Dave's dog Panther barked, and I followed the noise. Panther, a lab, circled the ladder that led up to the roof like he was trying to find a good place to sit. When he saw me, he came over and gave my leg a hump. It was our thing, I told Dave's parents whenever it happened in front of them.

"Don't worry," I'd say. "It's consensual."

They were Lutheran and didn't appreciate the joke.

The hatch was open, and I climbed up, cradling the case of beer against my side. Dave stood on the edge of the roof holding a piece of paper and staring down at it. There was no pizza to speak of.

If he heard me, he didn't acknowledge me, so I cracked two beers and walked over. He looked up when a beer can blocked his vision of the paper.

"Hey," he said.

"There's no pizza. You said there'd be pizza."

"Pizza will come. Chill," he said. "Work first."

I sighed and took a drink. It was only eleven thirty, but it seemed like a fine idea. I worked for a marketing firm and had just gotten back from a business trip to Seattle. It was my first day off in almost two weeks and I didn't care when I started drinking.

Dave handed me the paper. There was a grid pattern marked off in pencil and the words Welcome To Milwaukee written in the boxes in pen. He'd spelled

Milwaukee wrong and had crossed out the wrong letter. It looked like a botched crossword for kids.

"What's this?" I asked as I handed him back the paper.

"It's our project."

"Let me rephrase. Why is this our project?"

"We're painting it on the roof."

"This roof?" I looked around. I saw a faint chalk outline on some of the shingles.

"Yes, this roof." Dave tilted his head, finished his beer, and grabbed another.

"Why?"

"For the planes."

I raised an eyebrow. Dave had odd ideas from time to time—he had it in his mind until he was twelve that a raccoon would be a good pet—but this seemed a category all its own.

"We're in Minneapolis, you know that, right?"

"I know," he said.

* * *

We spent the better part of a six-pack each getting ready to paint. He'd lugged a few paint cans up already, but there were still more in the basement. He'd been buying them from a guy at the hardware store in the same plaza as his father's mechanic shop.

"They fell off the truck," Dave told me as I lifted two cans up to him on the ladder. He set them down and grabbed another two from me. None of the cans looked dented, but I still hoped he wasn't getting scammed too bad.

I was a little drunk by the time we'd gotten everything to the roof, and I thought about what it would feel like to fall off the side. I asked Dave about it, and he said not to worry, like he'd tried it before.

"You may break a bone or two, but you won't die. My father told me my grandpop fell off this roof when he was thirty and only broke a couple ribs."

"A couple ribs," I said, and thought of food.

Dave handed me a paintbrush. I felt artistic, standing up there, staring out over the river.

"Where do you want to start?" he asked.

"Milwaukee," I said. He nodded and clapped me on the shoulder.

"You got it, bud."

He'd pulled a replica of the design from his pocket and handed it to me.

"Start on the E and we'll meet in the middle."

I nodded. Dave picked up some of the empties and walked to the edge of the roof and looked down. In profile, I watched him lean over, close an eye like he was throwing a dart, and drop a can. It clattered off the asphalt. Dave leaned over more. I waited for the moment that he would drop, just be gone from view. I wondered if he'd yell, if there would be any notice other than his body not being there. I wondered how often he did this.

"I missed," he said. "I hate missing." He grabbed another can and aimed again. This time we heard the *tink* of metal on metal.

"Bingo," he said, pumping an arm. Dave remained leaning over, staring.

"Back up, dude," I said. He waved an arm in my direction.

"I'm fine," he said. "I like this."

*   *   *

I'd made it to the K when Dave abruptly stopped talking about the latest project he was working on down at the shop. I looked up. Dave stood, staring at a black dot. A plane was heading for us, growing by the minute. I went to say something and Dave shushed me. When the plane got closer, close enough to see the company's logo and the row of windows that looked like raisins from where we were, Dave began to wave. He waved for three minutes, until the plane had passed over us and, I assumed, made its way to MSP.

"Can they see you?"

Dave shrugged.

I didn't know what to say to that. I didn't know how to tell him that it was a stupid idea to wave to a plane. I'd done it once—on vacation in Florida—and my father told me it was a waste of time.

"Do you think anyone on that plane will want to see *you*, of all people, as they get ready to land?" he asked me. I was seven, in a pool, and he sat nearby with a bottle of Jack somewhat following my mother's orders to make sure I didn't drown.

"Yes," I said.

"Well, they don't. They want to see their loved ones, or a new place. If they're on vacation they want something new, they want a sense of adventure. Not some spoiled pale kid in a pool."

Dave had gone back to work. He'd about finished the first word before I'd made it halfway through mine.

"Why not Minneapolis?" I asked. The better part of the case was gone, and I was having a hard time holding onto the brush. I had to focus to keep a hold of it, and I had to squint to read the map. The sun, high above us like a sentinel, did not help.

"That seemed too boring," Dave said. "I want people to wake up when they get here. To live it up a little."

"I see."

"You know how it is, man. There's stuff here, but there isn't stuff. It isn't like Chicago or LA or New York. It's Minneapolis, a city that's mostly known for being a twin. It isn't even good enough to be known on its own."

He slapped a shingle with an open palm. "Why would people want to come here? This way, if someone's dozing on their way from, I don't know, Terre Haute or Boston or something, and the ride's been just fine this'll get their heart going."

"That seems mean," I said.

I wasn't paying much attention and had idly begun to paint a line of ants that trooped across the middle of the U. I looked up at Dave, but he didn't seem to notice. I tried to wipe it away with my hand which only served to make the letter look even worse.

"It isn't, man. Think about it."

I waited for him to continue, but realized after a minute of silence that he really did want me to think about it.

"I've thought about it. I've got nothing," I said. Dave stood and walked over to me. He had a crumpled beer can in his hand, which he tossed off the side of the roof, not aiming this time.

"I'm making people live."

"What if it's, like, a grandfather with a weak heart?" I tapped my chest.

"He'll be fine."

"Teenager with anxiety? Child flying alone for the first time?"

Dave waved my words away like clearing smoke after blowing out a candle.

*   *   *

We had just about finished when Dave got a call. His father, he told me after. There had been a wreck on 94 and he was going to have to stay late to start repairs.

"Big money client," Dave said, rubbing his fingers together in my face. His father had built up his grandfather's business, and they were known as some of the best mechanics in town. Dave had worked there since he was sixteen—eight years, now—and would take over when his father decided to let him. He changed the oil on every car I'd ever gotten.

"It doesn't matter that he's the owner," Dave told me once when he was drunk. "That fucker would rather be there than here. He wants me to do the same. He says if I don't, he's not going to let me have the business. He's going to cut me off completely. He says I can't let the family down like that."

Dave had closed his phone and sat on the edge of the roof, legs dangling. I sat next to him and turned my knuckles white gripping shingles. Dave didn't sway or wobble. His eyes were on the horizon. We sat mostly in silence, drinking. After a minute, Dave began to kick his legs and lean forward a bit. He still had a grip on the edge of the roof, but he moved like there was a heavy breeze. He said nothing, just rocked, and I watched.

The smell of paint mixed with whiffs of evergreen from the trees in the yard. The smell reminded me of cleanser, of freshness. I waited a few more minutes before speaking.

"You still haven't told me why," I said. "Like, really why you're doing this."

"Because," Dave said. "Because it helps me to get away. When I see a plane coming, just for a second I can pretend I'm anywhere that isn't here. Even if it's just Milwaukee."

He looked up. In the distance, we saw a plane as small as a bird, the engine drone preceding it on the light breeze. He stood.

"You know what it's like to know that you're never going to leave the city you grew up in?" He pointed a beer can at me, looked down at it, and pulled it back to his lips. Dave tilted his head back and drained it before tossing the can off the roof.

"You don't because you leave every other goddamn week."

I didn't say anything. What could I say? Dave continued.

"Exactly. You get the hell out and see the rest of the country. Coming back here is relaxing to you. You get to sleep in your own bed, eat your own food, masturbate in your own shower."

"I can't help that man, that's my job to be on the road."

"Yeah. I know. And my job? My job is to get oil on my jeans every goddamn day in the same goddamn shop in the same goddamn strip mall that my dad did, that my grandfather did. You think I want that? Why do you think I *still* have that world map on my wall?"

I hadn't thought of that map in years. Dave told stories about the pastel-colored countries that hung above us every time I came over as a kid. The stories were always adventures, and he was always the hero.

Dave huffed. He picked up the last beer, opened it, and drained it in one long swallow. The plane had gotten closer, louder, and I watched Dave's eyes lock on it as it approached.

"You can go somewhere. Take a vacation sometime, get out of town. Your dad will allow that."

Dave laughed. He broke off his staring contest with the plane's belly to lean over the edge again.

"Man," I said. I held a hand out. "Stop doing that."

Dave looked at my hand and spit off the roof. The empty can followed soon after.

I saw Mueller and Son becoming Mueller and Son and Son. I saw Dave's hands covered in oil and grime, not entirely clean until they give him one last sponge bath before embalming him. I saw the furthest place he'd ever go, a long weekend trip to a convention in Fargo. I saw everything when he looked up at the planes.

Dave resumed his position. The plane was almost upon us, its shadow floating over the land in front of us like a spectral whale. Dave's hands were on his hips and he squinted against the sun. His eyes reminded me of marbles. I looked up at the plane, wishing desperately that the map would stay up forever, that he'd keep telling stories. I wished for nothing more than one person—one—would look down and get scared, that their heart would beat into their throat and they would have to look at their itinerary, just to make sure.

THE RUSSIAN BRIDE
ANNA LEA JANCEWICZ

The slurry of dismal hours spent watching Saturday morning cartoons congealed into a brightly colored frenetic blob that lodged itself painfully just under Edie's sternum. She finally scooted off the couch, disentangling herself from all the girls' lazy limbs and all their piled blankets, with the excuse that she had to wash the breakfast dishes and mop the kitchen floor. But she didn't. She hovered at one of the side windows in the dining room, peering through the blinds for another glimpse of the neighbor's new wife. Edie had already seen the woman twice, and although it would have been the natural order of things for her to scurry right over with a plate of chocolate chip cookies to welcome a new resident on the block, this was a different situation. Unprecedented. The subject of much gossip. Their neighbor of six years, Tim, had acquired for himself what the mothers at the girls' bus stop had whisperingly reported was a Russian mail-order bride. Edie didn't know what to think about that. She'd never even met a foreigner before, let alone one who had been, presumably, ordered from a catalog to fulfill the marital dreams of a man, who after six years of owning his house, didn't have the decency to buy his own damn lawnmower.

She wore feathery earrings. Edie had seen her getting into Tim's pick-up truck Tuesday afternoon. Blue and yellow feathers that dangled from her ear lobes and swayed in the wind, mingling with her long blond hair. She'd had a cigarette clamped between her lips. Red denim shorts cuffed up to just below her butt, and Edie was pretty sure she'd been wearing flesh-colored nylons underneath. *Tacky.* But Edie couldn't help but think there was something glamorous about her anyway. Something exotic.

She found herself peeking out the windows between chores all Tuesday evening, and again the next day, and the next, hoping to see her. She caught just a flash of her crossing Tim's dining room as she set their own table for dinner Thursday night, and then nothing. Their truck was gone all day Friday, and then all Saturday, too. Edie had tried to just go about her business like normal, making banana pancakes and frying up bacon, snuggling in for the usual cartoon marathon, but she couldn't stop thinking about the woman. She was even more restless than usual watching the friendly magical creatures romp through enchanted landscapes and outwit black-hearted foes. She had no patience for superheroes or singing dinosaurs. Edie wondered if she spoke good English. She wondered if she knew how to cook American food. Maybe she would need somebody to teach her how to fry a chicken. Edie was somebody who knew how to fry a chicken, but had no idea what Russian people ate. Her veins felt tight in the backs of her hands and she couldn't concentrate. She broke out in a sweat while darning Billy's socks and had to get up and walk a circle around the back yard to get some air. She felt like she was going to crawl right out of her skin if she didn't see her again soon. And then she did. She saw much more than she had expected.

Edie got up late Saturday night to check on Delia, who'd been feeling feverish after supper and gone straight to bed. Billy had worked the day shift, but he was out again, probably at a bar. Edie was thinking about how he'd probably come home stinking sour and snore like a asthmatic grizzly bear, and need aspirins and sweet-talking to get him out of bed the next morning. She rolled her eyes in the darkness. As she paused at the end of the hall in front of the older girls' bedroom door, she glanced down out of the second story window and saw that the blinds were up and the lights were on in Tim's living room. Just a sliver of his couch was visible at that angle, but it was just the right sliver to see it all.

Edie had never before in her life seen two human beings having sexual relations. She'd seen R-rated love scenes, yes, but certainly never the real thing in person. She'd never even seen an honest-to-God *dirty movie*. But there they were, the Russian woman crouched on all fours and Tim, Tim with no lawnmower of his own, Tim who'd always complimented Edie's pecan pie so gushingly at every block party, was hammering away at her from behind, right in the middle of his living room. In the thirteen years they'd been married, Edie and Billy had never done it in the living room. They'd never done it with the lights on. Aside from that first time, that Wendy-making-time in the back of the Nova, they'd never done it anywhere but in their bed, under the covers.

Edie gasped in surprise and jumped back from the window. And then she leaned in to take another look. Her breath fogged the glass and she wiped it clear with her fingers. Her heart was pounding in time with Tim's furious thrusts. It didn't take long for them to finish, but then again, Edie didn't know how long they'd been at it. Tim got up and walked off toward the kitchen. From Edie's vantage, only visible from neck to knees. The Russian turned over and leaned back on the couch, plucking a tissue from the box on the coffee table. She spread her legs wide, one knee practically bumping her shoulder, and wiped herself.

Edie shuddered. It was so vulgar a thing to see. The gesture was bored, slatternly. Edie could just tell her eyes were fixed on the television as she did it. She was horrified. She dashed from the window, forgetting all about Delia's febrile brow, and shut herself in the upstairs bathroom, slamming the door and pressing her back against it. All of Edie's edges were frayed. She shut her eyes tight, but she saw it again and again. The Russian vagina. Fringed with dark hair. Yawning.

Edie had never even looked at her own before. They'd asked her, in childbirth, if she'd wanted a mirror to see the baby's head emerge, and she refused the offer each time, repulsed by the idea of it. She never even touched herself, it was true. She did what she had to do with Billy, but she just didn't have the inclination to go poking around on her own. Well, until that moment. Edie got down on her knees and started rummaging under the bathroom sink, looking for Reba's pink plastic My Little Pony hand mirror.

CUL-DE-SAC PASTORAL
MARCUS WICKER

*SELECTIONS OF THIS PIECE FIRST APPEARED IN SLIGHTLY DIFFER-
ENT FORMS IN* POETRY, PARIS AMERICAN, CINCINNATI REVIEW, *AND*
THIRD COAST.

The sill plays a cruel joke—thrones me. Frames me
Lording over lawnmower stripes—myself

in a shallow trench. In grass blades. Myself
persisting, despite a dickhead sun—me

in chlorophyll. Early, I find myself
swaying—me! in the black chokeberry, me!

in the rabbit's throat. Me, the rabbit. Me
dancing-out pellets. Out-dancing myself—

my father's pellet gun, the hawk. The joke
is a bright belly full of dark hopping

along my father's garden & the joke
small, between wrapped talons, is the hawking

too, is the axe sun, swift, rising, this joy.
This joy, it swallows itself far too soon!

                    *   *   *

This joy, it swallows itself far too soon
inside bright balloons, inside banquet tents

inside condiments, inside domestic
beer bottles, inside castled merriment

inside plastic champagne flutes raised skyward
for the neighbor's teen daughter, for he tents

his head, stakes it to the ground, every time
I wave. Help me—For his princess, he tents

her head when I'm inside my SUV
Kangol angled dangerous, so cleanly

cocked. For that, I should show the grad a mouth
of pearly. Merci, Neighbor. For your clean

cul-de-sac-arched mouth clamped, you Clampett.
(—) That. I should surely introduce myself.

                    *   *   *

That I should surely introduce myself
to the grill is important. For our guests.

Dear Broil King Master 490, found
you in consumers report on my own

then pitched you to Lisa. Love your 3 racks
ignition switch & spinning spit. Our guests

seem to love you too, especially Pete
with his wandering green eyes. But I own

your stainless steel vessel, your whoop-ticket
double burner system. That we are guests

here—your heat just reminded me. To stop
& smell the butterfly pork chops. We own:

deck, stained fence, city squirrel piss scent, not
you, god in Pete's eyes. You are flammable.

                    *   *   *

You, god in Pete's eyes, you are flammable
tender. My eyes are a faithful tender

yellow streetlight but this is the tinder
talking now. The nest—twigged, thorned, flammable—

& the ruffled black bird wants to know: What's up
with the burbs, its chemical lawns, tender

skinned children, its Uzi sprinkler heads? Down
the bowstring power lines blotting tender

twilight—it's the only way I'll leave. Flame
Buicks & midlife crisis sports bikes. Cleanse

this night. O, god in my eyes, you will flame
this cul-de-sac of plastic trash bins, cleanse

these driveways & if I enjoy & am
the view, Lord, can I still sit next to you?

AFTER THANKSGIVING
ELIZABETH KERPER

My father is reciting everything he knows about entropy
while he drives us home from Iowa to Illinois. The clouds
are a pale scrim across the sky, the cornfields reduced
to stubble and frost. My father explains that the universe
can only move from a state of order to a state of disorder,

that the laws of physics travel on a one-way ticket,
that this is why children know about growing up without being told.
Time is an arrow, he says, and entropy the bow that shoots it,
the reason we can never go back no matter how hard we try.
Even if you unburn the fire, unshatter the glass, scrub the kitchen,

end the affair, take back the lie, arrange all the books
in alphabetical order on the shelf, you will still store the confusion
somewhere else: in your lungs or the walls of your bedroom,
beneath the calm surface of a neighbor's swimming pool. He tells us this
and watches past the windshield as the highway sifts itself

through our tires. In the back seat, I think of my grandmother
behind us in Iowa, her immaculate house—drawers full of sheets
and dish towels starched and stacked in perfect fabric diamonds,
a silver rosary coiled on the bedside table, all the chaos
her tidy austere universe must be quietly unleashing on the larger world.

MIDWESTERN HAIBUN
CHARLOTTE PENCE

Loaves of white houses. Yards clobbered
into clods by horses. The waiting
animals lean over the waiting fences toward
wood fence, wire fence, steel fence, corn.
More corn. Browning between each rectangle
of home, each square of yard. Nobody here, we say
despite cars in the driveway. I am here, the sky
replies, long and lean, a sky that eats its veggies
and sleeps twelve hours each night. Here
in the middle of Mid-America, four-way stop
signs startle. Could there be anyone else?

We look again. White
hawk dives from the sky as road
pulls us in deeper.

Winter Visitor
SARA CROW

I was twelve years old on the January morning a doomed squirrel fell down our chimney.

He chattered the first day, scampering among the few square feet of space, slipping down the walls as he tried to clamber his way out. His first efforts didn't seem too urgent. Every once in a while, he'd stop and sit on the ironwork that held the logs above the stones, looking out into the living room with shining charcoal eyes, twitching the puff of his tail, probably feeling relief at being somewhere almost-warm. After all, it was -12 Fahrenheit outside and a balmy 50 degrees or so inside the fireplace.

But soon he realized he couldn't scale the walls and get back out the way he came in. He became panicked as hunger started to pinch his stomach.

Every time you walked by the living room, you could hear him, dashing and scratching. You could see flashes of his white belly and ochre fir as he scrambled around the space, but you couldn't see all of him at once anymore as he advanced toward the living room then dashed back toward the dark corners of the fireplace. Manic, until he passed out from exhaustion. His clawing made my teeth grind, but the silence of his fatigue left an anxious chasm, like the expectant gloom of an abandoned warehouse. My family tried to avoid the room, but it was on the way to everywhere. No friends were invited over to witness his throes. He was a dark family secret. Visitors were suddenly forbidden with an ashen flash across my mother's face, as if she was already touched by death.

He scraped against the glass door and the iron mesh, leaving streaks of blood on the surface, shining against the darkness inside the fireplace when it was wet, drying to a dull bark brown. I sat and watched, transfixed by his futile battle. My chest felt hollow. I was his only mourner. The rest of the family avoided him like he carried a contagious virus in his inevitable doom.

We called Animal Control. They told us to call back when he died and they would come take him away. They advised against trying anything else. Disease and parasites were a serious concern if he got loose in the house, they said.

One night I came downstairs after the rest of the house was quiet. The scritch-scratch-scratchscratchscratch preceded me, as if he were frantic to dig his own grave.

I put my hand against the glass, his clawing attempts at escape vibrating against my fingertips. I felt the hopelessness of his effort yawning inside of me.

Hot tears seared my cheeks.

"I'm sorry," I whispered against the glass.

Then, a furry THUNK against the doors. The chain grate slammed against the glass, cataclysmic in the silence. I stumbled back. I screamed.

My dad careened downstairs and swept me, convulsive and shrieking, into an embrace, pressing my face away from the scene.

Dad stood there with me in his arms in the dark living room and watched the last-ditch efforts of our incarcerated houseguest by the amber glow of the street-light outside as it shimmered across the snow in the front yard.

Crashthud. Crashthud. Crashthud.

His desperation sucked any more discussion from us. My muscles felt rubbery, as if I'd been fighting the flu for a week. Dad led me to bed and tucked me in with silent attention I hadn't experienced in years.

The noise had stopped by morning. Animal Control removed the empty body before noon. They insisted that he needed to be incinerated, in case he was rabid.

Windex on the doors removed the blood. A shop vac disposed of the rest of the evidence.

We had a fire in the fireplace the next weekend. I imagined the squirrel carcass flickering among the logs. Each pop was the water in the marrow exploding in the heat. Each hiss was flesh curling away from muscle. I could swear I smelled singed fur. For the first time I can remember, I preferred to do my reading upstairs in my bedroom.

A couple months later, an injured female robin fell down our chimney. The first sign of spring.

STARE DECISIS
GREG WALKLIN

The judge had already decided on leniency. The defendant's attorney, perhaps auditioning for the bench herself, sought the briefest possible sentence, concluding with a history of her client, a stick-thin defendant of fourteen, Miguel Ochoa. Lyman Walters, District Court Judge for Lancaster County, had already read the file, so most of the attorney's speech was redundant.

At trial, Ochoa had fought, and lost, criminal arson and vandalism charges. He had broken storefront windows and damaged cars and scorched an East Lincoln coffee kiosk. His attorney argued that it was retribution for his difficult upbringing, his shuttling from family member to family member, and his absent father, and thus his sentence should contain a measure of understanding.

Judge Walters used to love these hearings, especially whenever the better criminal defense attorneys—like this one—argued, though now he found them banal, as he generally entered with a fixed idea of the sentence.

"Is there anything else you would like to say for yourself, Mr. Ochoa?"

His attorney gave the boy a gentle pinch on the elbow.

"No sir," the boy finally said.

This, judging by the attorney's face, was not according to script. She motioned for him to stand up, but he either didn't care or didn't pay attention.

"Do you understand the sentence I am about to give you?" Walters asked, plodding through any confusion.

The boy nodded.

"You have to answer verbally for the court reporter," Walters said, even before Suzy, his dutiful scribe, could speak up.

"Yes."

"'Yes,' you understand?"

"Yes, I understand."

By now Walters had the standard recitations memorized, and all that needed to be appended was a discussion of the factors he considered in determining this sentence. He ordered Ochoa to complete a few hours of community service and pay a portion of restitution. The deputy county attorney stood in a shocked hush; having stuttered through his arguments in his creased suit, he must have been feeling that he had mucked something up—that perhaps it was indeed audacious to charge this kid as an adult.

Later that afternoon, on his way out, Judge Walters found the boy and a young woman standing outside the courthouse, off the front steps, waiting for him.

"Your honor," the woman said. "We just wanted to say thank you." It quickly became obvious that this woman, who was compact and authoritative, and likely too young to be Ochoa's mother, had engineered this encounter—the boy was two steps behind her and still sheepish, head still hanging low. "Miguel," she said. "I don't have much more time. I need to start packing."

Their handshake was clammy.

Walters was accustomed to cloying encounters—a brown-nosing attorney, a relieved former victim, irrepressible trial witness, juror, or, as here, a grateful defendant who had been given what amounted to a second chance, so perhaps it should have ratified something in him that he had made the right decision, that this boy was now venturing on a different path. But instead, as he walked to the parking lot, Judge Walters feared his guts had led him astray.

*   *   *

Over the last few years, sentencing had begun to make him uncomfortable—unease crept up over taking a man's (it was usually a man's) freedom away, dismissing all of his pleas of mercy, distinguishing whether his excuses were simple manipulations. Interpreting laws and statutes and rules of evidence were the enjoyable parts of his job. There were usually clear answers, or at least intellectual opportunities to find an answer. During sentencing, he needed to think of himself in the same way, as a cog, as a hand doing the work of a machine that was so large you couldn't see it—that he had to keep fidelity to principles that went beyond the circumstances of an individual case. "The law is not there for any individual person," the retiring judge whose place he had taken told him, "it's for everybody." He tried to tell himself he was just a lever, a pulley, a wedge, the end of a complicated series of functions. But did anyone just want to be a machine?

The governor had appointed him 20 years ago. He had been one of three candidates who passed the judicial nominating commission, composed of a coterie of his peers, who were supposed to select based on merit and qualifications, but ultimately made fairly base political decisions. Lyman Walters, Esq. appealed to conservative sentiments with frightening ease. His interview with the governor had been short and pointless. Near one of the mansion's four fireplaces, the cross-eyed governor had served decaffeinated coffee in beautiful old buffalo-themed china and asked Walters his thoughts on abortion, the death penalty, and whether he believed adhering to the actual language of the law and the original meaning of the Constitution. Besides guessing that perhaps caffeine made the crossed-eyes worse, Walters surmised in that moment there was nowhere less the governor wanted to be. To save money, he had delayed judicial appointments as long as legally allowed. Walters apparently gave him all the right answers.

A few years after he took the bench, he had attended a bar association event on juvenile justice to obtain the required continuing education credits, but mistook the starting time and arrived too early, just when the cocktails were being served. There he found a few old friends, counsel he used to litigate against, who were evidently already into a second round of cocktails. "Watch out everyone," Bert Landon had said, the laughter coming before the punch line, "the judge here will give you the chair if you say the wrong thing." Without intending, Walters had grown a reputation among the bar as a martinet. Soon after, the newspaper published an article about his hardline approach signaling a shift in a second "tough on crime" wave, and the governor called him to compliment his service and indicate that he was the model for future bench appointments.

Nobody told Walters, upon putting on the judicial robes, how all of his friends would change their conversations around him, how they would treat him differently. Even the longtime confidants—the ones he'd had since college, who remembered him passing out at a party, or caught him falling flat on his face going after a girl, or gave him advice when he was dissolutely smoking cigarettes all day and planning his motorcycle trip across the Badlands—all distanced themselves once they knew he had sentenced someone to death. The couples that he and his wife had socialized with would not get drunk around him. The secret meaning to "sober as a judge" was that you were a buzzkill at all parties. Not that he cared about being drunk—the post-trial hangovers where he'd felt his head unravel in the night which was never quite put back together the next morning, were awful—but it was comforting to see his friends slur their words.

Only his nephew Curtis, who had his own issues, had always consistently been the same, and only Curtis found other things—politics, movies, overdue library books—to talk about over backyard beers. When Curtis got the urge to get in shape and attempt, he said, "to turn his ship around," he would run the four miles to Walters' house, stop and say hello, with the intent to run back. But usually Curtis would hanker after a beer or two, and Walters would give in and drive him home. After Walters' wife died, Curtis stopped by more often; they both knew she had never liked his visits.

Curtis often wanted money, too, though never much, because it hurt his pride to ask for large amounts. Even with the judicial pay cut, Walters still lived comfortably, so he could always give Curtis some consideration. His salary was half of what he had been making as a partner at Bellton Jones, but he no longer had to kowtow to any corporate whims. And anyway, with his current circumstances, he no longer needed much. There were no college tuition bills to pay, no remaining mortgage, no medical bills anymore, and no furniture or household items left to purchase. His entertainment consisted of library books that Curtis had given him (returning them, Walters would pay the fine), or the newspapers. His groceries were basic. He hadn't any hobbies either. They had sort of dropped off gradually, like layers of an onion being peeled away, and the resulting working core that remained felt only more strong and substantive—as if giving up racquetball raised his legal acumen.

There was gardening, too, but that remained, perhaps, because it was essentially work. The butterfly garden was coming along; a few had already appeared, about on schedule, a Monarch and two Queens and even a Mourning Cloak. His wife, Willow, had originally built the garden, but after her death he could not shake the responsibility. Anyway, planting and fertilizing and weeding and watering and spreading mulch with his boots were when most of his opinions were actually written.

That's where he was, in the butterfly garden, watering and ruminating on a plaintiff's novel interpretation of the Administrative Procedures Act, when he noticed a small figure. At first, hearing the noise and sensing a person, he assumed it was probably Curtis, sweating and ready for a Miller Lite. But, looking up, there could be no mistaking Miguel Ochoa.

Ochoa didn't see Walters striding toward him until it was too late—until he had thrown the rock, with an apparent message attached, through the side living room window. It seemed ridiculous to give chase, but after the judge yelled at Ochoa to stop, and he didn't, Walters instinctively started running. When he nearly had the boy at arms length, ridiculously sprinting up the sidewalk past his neighbors (Who would be home? Who would see him?), it occurred to the judge that he very well couldn't tackle the boy; he couldn't trip him; he couldn't attack him. How would he explain it if he had to be in court?

It was so absurd he suddenly stopped. For a few seconds the boy kept up at full speed, and then, just as suddenly, halted himself. They exchanged a moment of silence before he took off again.

Back at his house, Walters took time washing his hands. The rock and the broken glass were in the trash and the folded-up paper on his kitchen table. It was a habit of his during judicial decision-making: hold off for as long as it takes to clear your mind, and once your mind is clear, you can start.

Go back and change my sentence and make me go to prison because if you don't do it there will be something worse than this rock, and yes that is a threat so write me up.

Walters considered reporting the vandalism to the police. But he knew well the Gordian Knot of papers, phone calls, meetings, and actions this would initiate, the long road of process and protection, of which he was one feature. Because of who he was, the police would investigate, and the county attorney would surely prosecute.

What kind of judge had he become, that he knew he wouldn't report it? He was now too wrapped up in the consequences, too wrapped up in the practicalities, to do anything other than explore the matter—to cut the knot—himself.

*　　*　　*

Academics and journalists always got mostly everything wrong about judging.

There were clear and wrong answers to the overwhelming majority of decisions he made. Lucid procedural rules, baseless arguments made by inmates, uncontested divorces. The academics and the journalists cared about the sliver that involved something else—and of that, the small portions that led to published appellate opinions. The law, like literature, was Hemingway's iceberg: the smallest rule was just the hint of a giant machination, a Rube Goldberg machine that spat out rights and evidentiary rules and administrative regulations. Depending on whom you spoke with, the answers to how judges decided things were through genetics, politics, egos, philosophical stances. Oliver Wendall Holmes, that great Solomon from more than a hundred years ago, had decided it was the person's guts that decided. Dworkin, by and large, agreed with him, at least as far as the Constitutional decisions went, and Posner was the guts theory's latest lion. Everything followed from the guts: the theories, the justifications, the factual spins, the principles.

And, after reading the note, Judge Walters' guts told him to look up Miguel Ochoa's address.

Although it wasn't far, the neighborhood was entirely different; the houses, more compressed together, lost bedrooms and garages and hedges and yard space. The right address was a house even more dilapidated than its neighbors.

Peering in from the concrete porch, he could see a woman apparently asleep on the couch inside. Even during several rings of the doorbell and a loud knock, she didn't stir. Walters was heading back down the weedy walk to his car when, from across the street, he saw Ochoa standing on the corner. They stared at each other for a few moments.

"So if prison was what you wanted, why did you fight the charge so hard?" he finally asked.

"That was my sister's idea," he replied. "Half-sister, really. She found the lawyer, too, got her to take the case for free. Guess it worked."

They stood in silence as a minivan passed, on the street, between them. His sister must have been the woman with him outside of court.

"I came to find out if you wanted to see what it was like," Walters said.

"For what?"

"To go to prison."

"For real?"

The judge nodded. "A sort of tour to see if you really want to spend any time there."

Ochoa obviously became less impressed the more he thought about it. "I get it," he said. "You're lucky I'm bored as shit right now. Otherwise I'd do just about anything else."

*   *   *

Life is a text, a book to be read after you die, which is how Judge Walters always thought of it and there must be a point, he figured, you can no longer redeem yourself and become a saint. Though he had sentenced, over the course of his career, two men to death—only one had yet been executed—it wasn't them he thought of often. Now, he thought of the more minor offenders. Instead he agonized over the young ones especially, whose lives were spiraling, the ones who perhaps had things left in them to do, the ones who wouldn't likely ever murder, but had been unable to extricate themselves from these spirals, from their deranged fathers or their addled mothers, from the lack of any parents, from sexual abuse, from the vagaries of the foster care system, from the sorts of daily hurdles that Walters would never have dreamed about—the boys (and occasional girls) who were at that corner, who could turn, the ones whose direction wasn't already set. There he wrestled with lenience. Like the boozy attorneys in town knew, he was a stubborn old martinet. If he were interviewed for the judicial appointment now, Walters was convinced, he would answer those questions differently—and that he would never get the position.

What would Willow have thought about him, sitting with this juvenile offender in his car?

On the way, Ochoa was fidgeting. "I know where the state pen is," he said. "It's just past the Burger King and the Amigo's."

"We're not going to prison," the judge replied. "At least not at first, and at least not the one you're familiar with. We're going to a house."

"You gonna rape me now or something?"

Walters just shook his head, and held up two fingers. "Scout's honor."

The judge pulled up in front of a blue Cape Cod in an old neighborhood lined with mature pin oaks.

"It's a shitty house," the boy said.

"It was always a shitty house," Walters said. "There was a boy who grew up in this house. He got into trouble often. By 'trouble,' I mean: fist fighting his teachers, vandalism, drugs and alcohol, getting an ex-girlfriend pregnant. He was suspended from school. He was eventually expelled, in fact. One night, he cut his own sister's hair in her sleep, snipping her scalp and waking her up. His parents tried everything to discipline him. They tried specialized counseling, medications, anything they could think of."

"Hold on," Ochoa said. "I get it. Let me guess, that was you and this was your home when you were a kid. Now you're a judge and wow, look at you..."

Walters smiled. "Try again."

Ochoa rubbed his hand over his face. "This must've been your dad? Brother?"

"No and no."

Ochoa just looked out the window.

"In response to the punishment from his sister's haircut," Walters continued, "the boy killed the family dog, a beautiful old German Shepard, and left it splayed in the front yard. The parents called the police, and they pressed charges against him. At court he attempted numerous times to represent himself, but eventually he acceded to a public defender. He was convicted, of course, animal cruelty."

"I'm nice to dogs," Ochoa said.

"No, no. This is something else—"

"I finally get it," Ochoa interrupted. "This was your son. This used to be your house."

Walters shook his head, smiling even more broadly. "Try again."

"Nah, you're just making this shit up."

"The boy spent several years in a juvenile detention facility. Perhaps he had some valid complaints about his mother and father. His dad was a high school teacher, at his son's own high school—or at least the one he went to for a spell—and coached every manner of sport. He was never home, but he was always at his son's school. His mother had a significant temper ever since she was a girl, and she was always unhappy. His sister was the only one who always forgave him."

With that last detail especially, Walters knew he had Ochoa interested. In his litigating days, his jury work, he was able to understand the precise grip he had on an audience, when he was losing them, gaining them, entrancing them. Ochoa was peeved, but he wouldn't have gotten into the car—or would have already left—if he was totally bored (A luxury most jurors did not possess).

They arrived next at a vine-ridden redbrick building, originally a soldier's home, which had first been repurposed into a juvenile detention center and then into a substance abuse treatment facility. The old building was the core of the new facility, and was redone years ago in a way that preserved the architectural motifs of the original Georgian architecture. Instead, Walters thought, it looked like the original home had been morphed into something spread out hideous with new wings—a pretty caterpillar turned into an ugly butterfly.

"He's still here," Walters said as they pulled into the parking lot. "This is no longer a juvenile center. He was here, he grew up, started drinking vodka and Sunkist every morning, he had to come back here."

"I bet he was a hard ass," Ochoa said.

"I wouldn't say that. He cried a lot. He could be released into family custody on the weekends, sometimes. He was a wreck. It wasn't stable."

"Just tell me who the fuck this guy is," Ochoa said.

"Maybe you want to meet him?" Walters asked.

"No."

"Well, I don't expect he would want to meet you, either."

By coincidence, a family was exiting the facility, a strung-out-looking mother and her two small blond copies. She had tattoos over her arms; the children had fake ones on their cheeks.

"He is my nephew," Walters finally said. "My sister had him when she was a very young woman. She married his father, eventually, a few years after Curtis was born. They've since divorced, did so not long after Curt was arrested. When he killed the dog, my sister didn't want him charged but Brett—my brother-in-law—did it without asking her."

"None of this shit is going to change my mind."

"It's only to tell you that you're like Curt in a way," Walters said. "He only had a mean soul for a time, but he's spent the rest of his life paying for it."

Ochoa didn't respond.

"So your sister," Walters said, thinking back on the day she and Ochoa approached him outside of court. "She was packing, I believe. She left town?"

"Texas."

"College?"

"Law school."

Walters turned off the car stereo. The blond children had been loaded up into a van, driven by a woman whose grey hair was pulled up in a bun, and the mother was walking back into the facility with her arms crossed over her chest.

Before he had ventured to Ochoa's house, Walters had read, again, the social workers' case summaries and the doctors' evaluations. None of them had said anything about Ochoa's sister, but they had said plenty about his family. His parents were gone but not dead. Of the two, his mother had stuck around a bit longer, being with the boy until he was about 18 months old, before handing him off to her brother. That brother handed him off to another brother and then to his grandmother, who was often ill, and who eventually decided she couldn't handle the boy and so desperately pawned him off to her missing son-in-law's semi-functional sister. His aunt was likely addicted to some kind of prescription pills, which made her sleep most off-and-on throughout the day; she was awake enough that Children and Family Services had never been able to pry custody away from her, despite their best efforts.

"So was this some sort of big show to get me to change my mind?" Ochoa asked.

The judge remembered the last time he visited Curtis here, the last spell Curtis had spent in the facility. It was the visit when he told Curtis that his aunt had died, and though Walters' wife had never liked the boy and the boy never took to Willow, Curt spontaneously cried and cried about it.

"I forgot to finish telling you about Curt's sister," Walters replied. Maybe this was what he had wanted to seize upon. "She ended up moving away, having her own family. Four children. Works as an advertising executive, and lives in Scottsdale, Arizona. She couldn't take custody of him. She was always going to have to live her own life."

The blond children had been loaded up into a van, driven by a woman whose grey hair was pulled up in a bun, and the mother was walking back into the facility with her arms crossed over her chest.

In silence, they drove to the state penitentiary, and found a parking spot from which they could see the yard. Men in khaki suits were milling about in the afternoon sun, some sitting on benches. Two caught sight of Walters and Ochoa and stared at them for a while before walking off.

"What makes you think this guy was anything like me? What makes you really understand anything about me?" Ochoa asked.

They were great questions, Walters thought.

*   *   *

She went by Willow because she hated both of her names, bestowed to her in honor of her female ancestors, who were all, Willow had said, "Wet rags." Women who stayed home and made pies every afternoon and were disinterested in voting, women who headed Edith Roosevelt's advice that "a woman's name should appear in print but twice—when she is married and when she is buried." Pie-making, or staying home were not anathema to Willow, at least as long as the path was actually chosen. But she knew enough about her great-grandmother Vera (first name) and her grandmother Louise (middle name) that she couldn't shake the conviction that neither had wanted to become masters of the kitchen. Vera was a painter; her great-grandfather converted their attic into her atelier, and in their house, and now in Walters' chambers, were many of her paintings, almost always seascapes. The woman could capture the swell of an ocean, a lake on a windy day, with striking precision. But she lacked the time and drive, Willow had always thought, to be professional; she only completed two or three paintings a year. Louise was a writer, and even closer to Willow's heart. Louise had typed novels in her dresser, in her nightstand, in her desk. Each one was a different genre, and after her husband died (her grandfather was a surgeon) she had even tried her hand at science fiction, a long tale about a roving medical starship.

The novels were nice stories, and the paintings beautiful. Willow loved all of them. What Willow couldn't forgive was the fact that neither Vera nor Louise had ever even tried to sell one. Maybe it was their fault or maybe it was the world. Either way, Willow was going to be different.

A voracious tree-climber as a girl, Vera Louise hardly ever came down. She went by "Bough" for a few months after her older brother found it amusing, but it was "Willow"—she was fond of a particular weeping willow tree, the only one she wouldn't climb—that stuck. Her long story on their first date, the way she apologized for her own name but explained her reasons, was what made Walters fall in love with her.

When she eventually told him she didn't want children, Walters readily agreed. A young associate at Bellton Jones at the time when they were engaged, he hadn't anticipated his life opening enough for a wife, let alone a child. Married, he still made partner, mostly thanks to winning a giant employment case that took him up to the 8th Circuit and back. The fees were astronomical, the client so pleased by the verdict that the firm had made a new decades-long revenue source. Her evenings alone, Willow had worked on her own pursuits—criticism and freelance journalism, profiles for some of the bigger general interest magazines and book reviews and essays on middle 20th century women writers, everyone whom Cather inspired.

Not long after her 50th birthday, doctors found a tumor swelling on her spine.

The tumor was impossible to remove; no surgeon would let them contemplate a miracle procedure, and anyway Willow would have died over and over rather than end up paralyzed. She was a climber, after all.

They spent many of the final evenings drinking bottles of good Shiraz, talking around the fire pit, paper lanterns swaying in the breeze, when it was warm enough to get by with a pullover or just a blanket. Enough Shiraz caused enough forgetfulness. But soon came her apologies, strange behavior for Willow. Sometimes they were general apologies for not liking a book Walters enjoyed, a cute neighborhood dog or cat, or a place they had vacationed, but eventually Willow began apologizing for everything she thought she had ever done wrong. There was more wine, and more apologies each night, then apologies for bigger things, more serious faults, even if they were old and already apologized for: the boy she briefly saw while Walters and her were dating. And he was busy studying for the bar; the times she lied about a girls' night out because she simply wanted nights alone, in a coffee shop or a bar; how she never particularly liked Walters' father and thought he had an illicit interest in her. Eventually Marla, the home health care nurse, would sit on the porch with them too, helping Willow get out of the deep porch chairs when it was time to come inside. But one night, towards the very end, Willow asked Marla to go inside before them, "not for my sake but for Lyman's."

"There was one thing I only recently realized I need to apologize for," she had begun. "Curtis." Walters hadn't understood. "I know what you really think. You don't have to say it. I shouldn't have let that dictate our choice not to have children."

She hasn't touched her wine, he remembered thinking. And that was all he could think, for the moments while he told her it was fine, that he didn't hate her, really, he didn't hate her, of course he didn't hate her. And even a few days later, he kept thinking of that full glass of Shiraz, glowing in the marigold lantern-light.

Every time Willow was reconsidering having children, every time she was actively saying she wanted a child, Curtis would do something particularly egregious. Eventually came a lull and a quiet celebratory dinner with Walters' sister and her husband when Curtis' medications seemed to have him under control. During that dinner was the only other time in her life Willow refused a glass of Shiraz. But the celebration proved premature. Curtis' medications weren't as effective as they thought and his behavior suddenly escalated, culminating in killing the family dog, which a pregnant Willow found when she stopped over to drop off leftovers. The death of the dog, whom Willow had always been fond of, had imprinted itself inextricably on her. It wasn't due to the dog, of course, at least not entirely, but she miscarried a few weeks later. The night they had returned from the hospital, as Willow and Walters lay in bed, mostly silent with the lights turned off, she said, "It was probably for the best, anyway."

* * *

A few weeks after Walters showed Ochoa the substance abuse treatment facility, he received a late night phone call from the police. Curtis had fallen, or perhaps jumped, from a downtown overpass.

His fellow judges helped as they could, taking an administrative appeal or two, or a few no-property divorces, cases they could move through quickly. Curtis survived the fall although he suffered significant brain damage, the extent of which it wasn't yet clear; the doctors had put him in a coma in the hopes of mitigating future harm. Walters volunteered for the job of cleaning out Curtis' room at the center, which was unpleasant for many reasons, none of which he planned on telling his sister. He also attempted to get in touch with his niece in Arizona—she and her mother never spoke anymore—but she didn't answer his calls or emails.

Until he came across a particularly dismaying case, his return was smooth. But when he was assigned one case in particular by lottery, he thought about recusing himself, and he continued to think about it until the prosecutor informed him that the defendant was planning to plead no contest to the charges. The county attorney had, based on the defendant's record, refused a plea deal. Walters kept intending to recuse himself, and he should have, but something kept him from it. Sitting in his chambers the day before the sentencing, he thought of a study of butterflies, which he'd come across in a magazine a few days before, during an afternoon working in the garden: even after the chrysalis and even after having melted down into goo during their transformation from caterpillars, butterflies showed evidence of remembering their life on the ground. Despite all the transformation, a core memory—in some form—still remained. Would it be the same with Curt, if he ever came out of the coma?

Whatever it was inside him telling him how he should treat this new case, he was bound by it, by what had come before.

On the day of sentencing, Ochoa's sister wasn't in the courtroom this time; a public defender was representing him. It was the only time in his career, Walters believed, that a defendant smiled at being sentenced the maximum.

PAPER COMES FROM BIRCH TREES
HENRY HEIDGER

There's a house
in the moonshine valley.

The licks of paint are peeling
like paper birch.

Can't tell what color it used to be.
But the house can still stand on two feet.

When I was young, my mother said
all paper comes from birch trees.

The beautiful lie
of imagination. A quick gift.

The branches are hand models
displaying wares, showing off

glass trinkets. Bottles hang in the trees:
hollow little ghosts, blue,

brown and green. They sing
in the wind like children sing.

The old woman is alone. She tells me
her husband is coming home

soon. He's alive enough to talk to.
She hangs bottles from branches

like little ornaments. They chime
out of earshot, out of mind.

FINDING A USE FOR THE WORD DOUR
LISA J. CIHLAR

My mother took a photograph of my father in his casket. It seemed weird to me then; it seems weird to me now. I never saw it after it was developed. When she dies and we are going through her things, I do not want to find it stuffed in a bed-side book, or tucked under the giant paperclip holding notes and coupons by the wall-mounted telephone. The phone with the long cord that reached halfway up the stairs to the unheated bedrooms. Meant to give a sense of privacy, but there was always a small echo and the chance that a sibling or teasing parent might listen in and make fun of my secrets, no matter how banal they might have been.

The face of a man in a coffin is pinched and powdered. Not the grinning co-median holding babies, or puppies, or just-caught fish with equal delight. In the cedar chest inherited from my grandmother, I found a death photo of my great grandfather. He looks too dour to be related to the rest of us.

HALF AS HOLY
GARY DOP

For the eternity of 1985, I didn't wash
my forehead after her Mary-like lips sung
on my pubescent skin. The pastor's wife,

Amy's in-law, invited the church kids
to the post-concert party in Harker Heights.
Amy kissed me under game room lights

'cause I blurted, *My name's Gary,*
like your husband. She smiled.
My forehead puckered. On a Friday

years later, the radio said that Gary
and Amy were no longer one. She'd sinned,
I concluded, like Eve finding some snake's

apples to bite. I broke *Lead Me On*
into fifty mirrored pieces and tried
to forget the 7th commandment

written in stone. Then Mom called
and whispered about Dad and the way
continents shift apart. I wrote Amy

to apologize for everyone who had held stones.
When she didn't write back, I downloaded
Unguarded from Napster and never listened.

I keep her on my hard drive,
a bad file buried under nameless folders.
Amy Grant kissed me. I wish

I were half as holy again.

DELUGE
LISA MECHAM

I wonder about the old man bagging groceries, packing my purchases just so. A puzzle he's pleased to complete each time. He never speaks. He is, as we used to call it, slow. Beneath whispers of white hair, tributaries of blue, his skin sags. A washcloth wrung out too many times. By the way he walks, heels heavy, he might be missing toes.

On these nights alone, kids gone and rarely in touch—the new order of things—I consider catastrophes. Settle on his generation and geography: 1927, unending rains bloat the Mighty Mississippi and she overflows her forks, her feeders. One thousand miles long, eighty miles wide. Just a boy, he makes his way to the river's edge, mouth agape. Its path no longer a meander, but the stake of a claim.

He wades in, the current's tendencies newly endowed. Destructive. The muck, the river's throat, seizing his feet. He cries out as water rushes in. A yapping dog, a father, a rope. Despair in the grass where he's laid out. Never the same. Forever slung between miracle and disaster.

The next time—amid banging carts, unruly kids, mothers with their phones and lists—after he places the sleeve of spaghetti on top of the eggs, before he lifts the bag into my cart, perhaps, I will take his hand. With his body and mine, we might remember. A child's tiny hand pulling mine, *Momma, come see!* A father's cupped palms pumping his chest with each *please, please, please.* What we meant to them before.

THE TINY WOODS
LINDA NIEHOFF

Neil didn't want to go. He stood under the damp purpling sky, his gaze falling to the woods like it always did. The tiny woods, they had called it, because it wasn't the real woods. More like a stand of trees at the edge of the gravel drive that, for some reason, had been mowed around all those years ago instead of mowed over. They had let it grow shaggy and wild and untamed. Behind him was the gray house with a front porch that sagged like an old mouth gone slack. The house stood on an acre of open field except for that clump of trees.

He'd sealed the keys in a manila envelope and would drop them in the mail on his way out of town. He'd already boxed up the last of his childhood—his first baseball his teammates had signed in crooked letters, the gray teddy bear missing an eye, and the school papers he'd written in lopsided handwriting. All of it was stacked and sorted, tossed and boxed, and carried past the sold sign in the yard and slammed shut in the trunk of his car, which now hummed next to him, waiting. He had a reservation at a Best Western two hours from here. Then he'd drive the rest of the way tomorrow. But Neil didn't move. He watched the woods. And he didn't want to go.

"It's haunted," his mother told him more than once about the tangle of trees. His dead mother. He winced like he'd been punched. He wasn't used to it yet. His mother, who'd been the wind and sun and haunted stories that shivered in his bones when she tucked him in and flipped off the light, was gone. The woods had been just another one of her stories. Still he wouldn't go into them. Not for any dare in the world.

He once suspected that children disappeared in those woods. When their mothers called them from evening doorways, they never answered. Their names hung, forever suspended on the twilit air. He had no proof other than childhood certainty. Those woods ate things.

Neil could remember being very little and could remember how they tossed his old car seat made of black vinyl and metal down a long dark hole.

"It was the dump," his mother told him later. He asked on a day when she could still remember who he was. But he'd always thought that it was taken to the tiny woods—that all of his childhood playthings were drug out one by one and fed to the earth and to the trees. Later in the dark, he imagined tendrils of roots wrapping around and pulling each thing down into its soft brown belly. It slowly ate his childhood piece by piece. That's how he remembered it.

The last few weeks, he'd studied its outline from an upstairs window. The trees looked like black lace against the almost-evening sky. They were almost pretty.

He turned around only when his mother moaned and shuffled in her bed. Sometimes she didn't recognize him. Other times, the edges of a pale smile appeared. A bony finger plucked at his short hair once when he bent down over her. "You look different," she said. Her voice was fragile like a broken piece of china. Then her eyes looked past him. "Where's Neil?" she asked. Then more frantic, "Where's my boy?"

"I'm right here." He said it aloud now in the driveway to the wind that picked up. But he didn't quite believe himself. He was afraid that if he looked down at his feet, he'd see that he was transparent; that time was moving so quickly it was pulling away from him. That's how it felt. All of it was moving too fast.

He ran a hand through his clipped hair, along his sandpaper cheek. She was right. He was different. The black suit he wore now wasn't just for the funeral. His whole world was made up of black funeral suits. He'd cut his childish curls years ago. His skin was no longer boyhood brown from the sun. And he no longer believed the woods were anything other than an old clump of trees. That was his fear now. That it was only a story.

Sometimes when he saw that pale smile of hers, he'd say, "Tell me another story."

"About what?"

"The woods."

She'd close her eyes as if it was too much effort and mumble, "Don't go in. Even if it wants you to. And it does. But you can't ever let it have you."

Then she was gone to sleep and to days of not knowing. Of asking for him even as he stood by her, holding her hand and telling her shhh, it would be alright.

If he could just stand here a moment longer. That's what he'd wanted those past few weeks looking out the window. That's what he wanted now. The sold sign meant bulldozers would come with their open jaws and tear it all apart. The woods, the house, all of it. It had stood at the edge of town and now town was creeping in closer until finally it couldn't be kept away anymore. Not even by the woods.

"It's not haunted," he had told himself a hundred times at three a.m. when vines and leaves and branches crept under his eyelids and curled into his dreams, and he'd sat up cold and shaking, feeling like he'd just let go of something he was desperate to hold on to. "It's not haunted," he'd whisper with only the dark to listen. It was just a story she told when he was a boy, and in his childish bones, he had believed it. But not now. It couldn't be.

But the dreams. Hadn't they meant something? What if it was haunted? What if it did devour? What if you went in and never came back out?

He moved toward the woods.

That familiar dark shiver ran through him. Hundreds of times he'd stood at its edge, pushing his face between the branches, trying to see without going in. Just as he did now. But it was hard to make out anything in the draining light.

Maybe if he went inside, his name would be called on the evening wind by someone not yet gone to their own grave, and he would never answer. Just disappear. Then he would be suspended with all those childhood things. All of what he'd lost.

It was crazy to think that way. There was no such thing. And yet, somewhere under his veins that tiny knowing trickled through him still. How did anyone believe anything? God? Or love? How did anyone really know?

He turned around. Raindrops now fell in heavy silver streaks against the car's headlights. There was no wife. No kids. Nothing to stop him. Just the car idling behind him. Just a reservation two hours away.

The worst thing would be that he'd walk in and nothing at all would happen. He'd walk back out the same as he ever was. He'd drive the two hours to his motel and then the rest of the way tomorrow only to drown in a world of dark suits. Either way, he had to find out for sure.

One last glance, one last look at the sagging gray house, at the car that still idled. One last breath, then he turned back to the woods. He could almost see it now. Those crooked limbs reaching out like arms. The way the entire clump of vines and branches and papery leaves seemed to wait for him. Had always waited for him. He almost hoped for teeth as he reached out, pushed the branches aside, and stepped in.

DIRT
RACHEL RICHARDSON

Jimmy dug. He'd been digging all morning, one trowel-full at a time. He was hot, so he went inside for some Kool-Aid and cereal. The hole was getting deep.

The pliers Uncle Boots had used on Mama soaked in a pan. Jimmy didn't know where the teeth were. He pulled the Kool-Aid pitcher from the fridge and rinsed out a bowl. The cereal was mostly dust. Jimmy had to stand on tiptoe to reach the sink. He found a plastic spoon still in its wrapper from the pile on the stove and went in the living room.

Mama and Uncle Boots slept with the TV on. The couch was brown and orange, floral. An old sheet tacked to the window kept the light dim; a fan blew, turning slow. The television only got one channel. Jimmy twiddled the rabbit ears—some show about China and the pandas that ate bamboo there, but the colors were all wrong. The bears were red and yellow, then ultraviolet tinged with green.

Jimmy had to clear a spot on the low table to set the pitcher down. He pushed aside the ashtrays crammed with Uncle Boots' smelly Monarch cigarettes and Mama's favorite tumbler, a gas station cup that said ALL I EVER WANTED WAS EVERYTHING. He was careful not to touch the glass pipe or the baggie of powder, the blue Bic lighter, and the tin foil. Beer cans with the tabs snapped off made a ring around the cough syrup.

Mama slept with her mouth wide open, and Jimmy could see the empty spots where her teeth had been. They'd been gnawing at her for days, making her cross-eyed with pain, so Uncle Boots found some pliers and took them out for her. Jimmy hoped it helped; maybe Mama would get up and make him some butter noodles or a ketchup sandwich for dinner.

He ate his cereal and watched the TV. A panda reclined on his haunches, mechanically chomping away at bamboo stalks. An old man narrated: *The giant panda lives primarily in the Sichaun Province, but can also be found in the Qin Mountains of Shaanxi.*

Jimmy set his empty bowl on the floor and went back outside.

Jimmy dug. The sun was hot and high overhead. Cicadas screamed in the trees. The old mad dog tugged at his chain, barking. Under the trailer, the new kittens mewed.

The little girl stood by the pile of scrap metal Uncle Boots had hauled from the Pick-N-Pull car yard up in Maxwell. She wore the same purple dress with pink rickrack, her yellow hair clumpy around her ears. Bug bites dotted her skinny legs. She was seven, maybe. Her teeth were gone in front.

She'd been coming by for days now, just standing around and watching Jimmy as he hunted for grasshoppers or threw sticks at the old rusted car propped up on blocks. Jimmy didn't mind. She was a baby, sure, but she was the only other kid around. In his head Jimmy pretended she was his silent sidekick. Her name was Hannah or Shannon or something.

Jimmy wondered whether she'd gotten any money from the tooth fairy. One time he'd found a whole dollar underneath his pillow and hid it in the waistband of his Spiderman underpants. That was back when Daddy still lived with them, before Uncle Boots moved in. Jimmy had a piggy bank, too, until the day Uncle Boots smashed it, hollering about how there weren't nothing but goddamned pennies and buttons inside.

Jimmy waved the little girl over. She squatted by the hole and stuck a finger up her nose.

"I'm digging a hole to China," Jimmy said. The idea struck him sudden, a flash of genius. "Go get you something and we'll get there quicker."

She took off again. The soles of her feet were black. Jimmy remembered how Daddy used to wash his feet before bed, the wet rag rough along his toes like a cat's tongue. He'd asked him one time why he did that—nobody else he knew had their feet washed before bed. "Couldn't say, son." Daddy had unfolded and refolded the rag, making a damp square. "Just habit."

The little girl came back with a pie server. She crouched down and stabbed at the earth.

They dug all afternoon.

Jimmy talked. "My Daddy's in China. He's saving the pandas. He's probably in a bamboo jungle right now fighting a python." Jimmy shoveled and the little girl jabbed away with the pie server. "We got to go get him, though. He'll have a treasure chest full of emeralds and rubies. And he'll be wearing a hat. And he'll have a gun."

The little girl kept digging.

"And when we bring him back, we'll all go up to Diamond Jim's and get all our stuff back. The lawnmower," he said. He wiped the sweat off his forehead, trying to remember all they'd pawned. "My remote-controlled racecar. And we'll go to Disney World. And I'll get a hamster, and get one of those plastic houses with the tunnels and the wheels. I saw it on TV once. A Deluxe Hamster Habitat."

Jimmy rambled on and the mad dog kept barking, tugging and snarling.

The light got long and orange and they were still nowhere near China. Jimmy dug faster, dirt flying over his shoulders, his discarded t-shirt buried and filthy. They'd never make it. He held out his hand and the little girl stopped. They stood over their hole and thought.

"What we need," said Jimmy, "is an elevator."

The little girl looked up at him. A fine film of grit darkened her face.

"I'll be right back. You stay here and guard this."

Jimmy handed her the trowel and set off, searching for a box. He weaved between the trailers, scouring, but all he saw was junk: lawn flamingos and wind chimes and Big Wheel tricycles all faded from the sun. Garbage sacks of cans. An old mattress with springs popping out. Jimmy was about to give up when he spotted it—mostly intact, still with some plastic packing tape on its edges. It was too small for him, but she'd fit just fine.

Jimmy pulled it free and ran back to the hole. For a second, he thought she'd ditched him, but then he saw her bottom sticking up as she looked under the trailer. He shouted at her.

She turned to him, baby cats in each hand. "Kittens," she said.

"Here, look." Jimmy set the box inside the hole. He fished a crayon he'd been keeping in his pocket and drew two arrows. The little girl stood over him, kittens squirming in her arms. "See, you just push this and then you'll go straight down, all the way to China."

The kittens mewled.

"Well," said Jimmy. "Go on."

She handed off the kittens and dropped down into the box. She sat and held out her hands. Jimmy gave her back the kittens. She made a tent of her skirt and set them in the hollow of her lap.

"It's dark," she said.

"It won't be dark in China," said Jimmy. "You just push that button, okay?"

She nodded.

Jimmy folded the flaps back over and pushed the dirt over the box's top. He filled in the hole until it was level again. Mosquitoes buzzed in his ears. Jimmy tamped down the earth until it was smooth, satisfied with knowing that at least one of them was on their way to China, that his Daddy would be there soon. And and then he went inside.

PRESAGE, THE BODY PROPER
RYAN DZELZKALNS

Minneapolis has been cut by the river.
　　When we lived there
we were like two shores pressing against each other. And to think
　　　　　　we only climbed the buildings once.

　　I liked watching movies with you because you always　　　　fell asleep.
　　　　Your breathing would slow and you would twitch as you disappeared
　　　　　　　　like you were dying.
　　I would press my face against your chest
hoping the movie would never end.
　　　　　　　　　　That winter
　　　　your windows coated themselves with ice,
　　　　　　you were so sick,
　　　　your throat so swollen, you stopped breathing like an open door.
　　　　　　　　　　In the E.R.
　　they lanced your throat to drain the pus
　　　　　　　　　　two wounds
　　　　like rivers left open in the back of your mouth.

The first time I told my father about you　　I asked him to prescribe me antibiot-
ics.
　　　　　　　　　　You were always so sick.
　　　　Even when you came to New York, I had to wash
　　　　　　the towels and the sheets.

You're still in New York but we don't speak, the East River between us.

I remember once we could walk around an entire lake,
　　　　　　　　　　eat a box of donuts, bike on the highway.

　　　　　The last thing you said to me
　　the MRSA sprouting braille across my thigh: SOS

mayday
mayday
mayday

VIEW OF THE FAIRWAY
LEE COLIN THOMAS

They'd been walking; it was something to do

at sixteen when evening skimmed
across the Minnesota prairie
to their little college town. A cottony wind

swept the humid hours away
with the late-waning sun.
She called after dinner. He left home

and turned toward hers, walked past
flickering television-lit windows, laugh tracks
blending with cricket calls, until he saw her

under an ochre cone of lamp light
on a sidewalk halfway in between.
They talked low and wandered

along the edge of the golf course,
took each other's hand and ventured
step by step into darkness.

Across temporarily abandoned lawns,
up to a little rise on the 16th tee
where they sat and watched

shadowy shapes of trees on sable grasses
overlap in a sooty collage of construction paper
scenery, scissor-fringed pine branches

waving in the pitch, star-flecked
glitter on the page and moon-glow
pooling like glue in the sand traps.

They fell asleep there, paperclipped
together on the grass. They did not dream
of the future, of the damage and joy

that would be drawn and torn
in the space of another decade or two.
They woke to daylight

and a whole world
cut from fresh sheets
of yellow, blue and green.

TRESPASSING
WENDY A. SKINNER

John Reid got the call early one November morning, just like any other. Routine trespassing. Or so it began.

"My property's posted," said Dan Knutson, a small-potatoes logger, over the phone, his deep voice indignant. "But somebody's got a trap line on it."

"Where can I meet you?" John asked.

"The end of my driveway. It's south of town on 27. Right-hand side just before the Indian reservation." He paused and added gruffly, "I gotta wolf, too. Live. In a snare."

Not so routine.

"And I'm not having nobody point a finger at me for taking a wolf between seasons," he insisted. "They aren't my traps."

"I'll be right out." John rubbed the knuckled stump on his left hand where he'd lost three fingers years ago in a domestic violence call. He looked at his watch. 9:12. He sopped up the last of his eggs with a corner of toast and grabbed his jacket with Conservation Officer printed in gold letters on the back.

On the way out, he locked the front door. No one else around here locked their doors, but it was a habit from the city which he could not let go. What if on his return he surprised a drug addict who had taken advantage of the open door, looking for cash and guns? A crime of convenience. A preventable confrontation. Ten years on the Minneapolis police force did that to a person, etched into his brain the violent possibilities of *what if?*

Outside, the sky shone an intoxicating clear blue, but the frigid air sobered John up and he pulled his black knit cap over his balding head. Armed with his .223 rifle on the rack, a 12-gauge under the seat, and a laptop computer mounted on the console, he drove his pickup south through Superior National Forest, past Greenstone to the Knutson place.

John left Minneapolis after losing his best friend, his fiancé, and his hope that he'd never have to kill anyone. He gladly accepted the position of game warden in this remote corner of northern Minnesota, a dozen miles south of the Canadian Border. The small, isolated mining towns, smatterings of glacial-scraped lakes, and forested wilderness gave him spaces in which he could breathe. After more than a decade as a conservation officer—that's what they called game wardens nowadays—he still welcomed the daily tedium of his 24/7 routine. Enforcing game laws was more like public relations compared to the life and death situations that came with armed robberies, road rage, gang shootings, and domestic violence calls, his least favorite of them all. Not that he liked confronting any desperate person, but when it came to affairs of the heart, well, no one could predict what a person was capable of until love or jealousy tested him.

*   *   *

Five miles down County Road 27, John found the end of the Knutson's driveway deserted.

He turned in and drove a quarter mile through the pines past a black spruce-filled bog. On a rise above the bog sat a log house with a squat roof surrounded by a thick stand of pines. The sun peaked over the treetops, casting long purple shadows on the snow. As he got out of the truck, the smell of burning birch filled the air. A lazy wisp of smoke rose from a stove pipe poking out of the cabin roof beside a TV satellite dish. John's *what-if* radar sharpened.

It was quiet. Too quiet. He imagined the same stillness in the air years ago when his best friend Keith, a fellow officer, found the *slumper*. The man was sleeping in a car in a North Minneapolis church parking lot. A routine call. A warrant was out for the slumper's arrest, but before Keith could reach the squad car to look up the man's record, he took three bullets in the back.

"Hello?" John knocked on the front door. The busted-out screen rattled. "Hello!" He rubbed his knuckles and counted to ten before following a worn trail through snow and trees to the backside of the cabin.

"Inside my heart there's an empty room," a mournful voice sang from inside a small pole barn. Young and feminine, the voice cut through the winter stillness like a siren over a frozen sea. "It's waiting for lightning. It's waiting for you..."

"Hello?" He raised his voice as he knocked on the barn door and stepped into the darkness. Before his eyes could adjust, the smell of warm hay and summer pastures filled his senses.

A young woman popped up from behind an interior pen. "Oh!" she cried, a startled expression on her face. Under a blue knit cap, a long blond braid snaked over her shoulder. Her pale blue eyes were red and swollen.

"Someone called about trespassing and a wolf? A Dan Knutson?"

"Jesus," she said and looked away, down toward her hands where she held clumps of hay. "Didn't Danny meet you at the road?" Two goats no taller than her knees milled about beside her snatching mouthfuls of fresh hay from the floor. Rays of sunlight streamed in through a small window igniting dust particles in an aura around her.

"No, he wasn't there." He held out his hand. "I'm John Reid."

She dropped the hay, wiped at her face and shook his hand. "Bijou. I'm Danny's wife."

When his eyes met hers, it took only a moment for his heart to quicken. Yes, he was sure. He recognized her kind.

*   *   *

"Turn right here," Bijou said, pointing to a logging road in front of a colorful wooden sign announcing the entrance to the Indian reservation. "Dan freaked out about the wolf. I should've known he wouldn't meet you."

John drove the truck past tattered, barely legible *No Trespassing* signs.

"You can tell Dan to prosecute a trespassing violation he needs a signature on these," John said. "A phone number is a good idea, too. Otherwise there's no way to know who posted them." Public relations also meant education. "Last year I came across a dozen brand new no-trespassing signs posted just off the end of Broad Axe Trail. No names. Just blank."

"Broad Axe? Isn't that—"

"Yeah, the Boundary Waters. It's an old trick some trappers use to cut out the competition. They basically claim a private trap line on public land. Of course, it's illegal. And on a federal wilderness? I'm guessing they'd get more than a slap on the hand, but that'd be the Feds' call to make, not mine." Funny how that kind of thinking got some people in trouble here. They could get real possessive about their wildlife and public lands on the Iron Range. They didn't want to share it with any outsiders—especially *packsackers*—canoers or anyone else from the city like John. If you weren't born on the Range, working the iron mines or harvesting the timber, you'd always be a *packsacker*.

Bijou kept quiet as they passed a patch of stumps and fresh slash every now and then.

"This seems like a lot of bother to trespass for a few traps," John said when they came to a dead end at a frozen beaver pond. He put the truck in park and turned the ignition off. He assembled his shotgun and pocketed a couple of shells. "Just in case," he said. They got out of the truck to walk the rest of the way. Bijou led him on a trail south and perpendicular to the logging road, even deeper into the woods.

"No one's been here but me since it snowed a couple days ago," she said.

Another violation. Not surprising. You couldn't expect a trespasser to check his traps and snares every 24 hours as required by law.

"There she is." Bijou pointed to a game trail that cut between another pond and the bottom of a steep slope.

A wolf lay on its haunches in a matted patch of snow. It lifted its head, straining at the cable noose and looking at them like the Sphinx, its eyes burning two amber holes into its coal-colored fur.

John's skin tingled. The wolf's cold stare went right through him. He stepped closer and the wolf averted its gaze. The snare was buried deep in its fur, but the wolf's trachea must have held up because the animal appeared alert. Usually as soon as the animal struggled, the snare tightened and cut off circulation until the animal either passed out or broke its trachea, causing it to suffocate. This one was lucky.

"Poor baby," Bijou said. "You're not going to shoot her, are you? That was the whole point of bringing you out here, you know. I figured you'd free her, not kill her."

"No, I'm not going to shoot her," John reassured her. "And if I did, the only reason would be if she were suffering, and she's not—yet—not like some animals I've seen. Last year someone set a 220 Conibear for a coon within Greenstone city limits. That did not turn out so well for a border collie. Come on." John turned around and walked back to the truck. "I've got an idea of how we can get it out."

They returned carrying the metal ramp John used for loading his snowmobile into the truck bed.

"We're going to lay this down on top of her," he said as they walked up close to the wolf. "No big deal. Just nice and easy so I can cut the snare."

"You sure about this?"

"Trust me." This was his first live wolf and he wanted to keep it that way. There wasn't much time. If this had been three years ago, before the state started managing wolves, the wolf might have died waiting for Federal Wildlife Services to come out with their bag of tricks.

John and Bijou lowered the ramp onto the wolf, pinning the animal to the ground. John reached through the grate and snipped the cable at its neck.

"Slow and easy now," he said. They lifted the ramp off and set it aside. The wolf laid there, so docile John could have reached out and rubbed its silver belly as if it were his own dog. The wolf stood and took a few steps. Bijou sucked in her breath. It sniffed the air nodding as if thanking them, and trotted away through the underbrush.

John's heart beat double time. "Whew," he exhaled, and sat in the snow. Bijou dropped down beside him. She rested her face in her hands.

"First I begged Danny not leave her out here to die," she said. "Then when he left the house with the shotgun I told him if he didn't call you, I would."

"Hey, it's done," John said. "The wolf's free. How is it you found that wolf in the first place?" Something did not feel right about this. "And what about the other traps?

Bijou kept her hands over her face.

"Dan said the trespasser had a trap line."

"Most of them are buried under the snow," she mumbled into her palms.

"What? You've seen them? You have an idea of who's been setting them?"

She shook her head. He waited for her to fill the silence. Then she nodded and sighed.

"They're *his* traps. *His* trap line. When he doesn't get around to checking them, I check them the next morning. I hate it." Her hands dropped. Her face had flushed with anger. What she said next fell from her mouth like water breaking through a beaver dam. "He didn't mean to catch that wolf. The snares are set for fox—a lousy 25 or 50 dollars a pelt. Says we need the money. But I'm already working two jobs, the bookstore during the day and the nursing home at night.

It's not like we're starving. I don't know where he spends it all." By the time she stopped, her voice had dwindled, as if a snare had cinched itself tighter and tighter around her neck.

"So let me make sure I understand this right," John said. "There is no trespasser?"

She nodded her head.

"Does Dan have a trapper's license?"

She shook her head. "I shouldn't have said anything." She pursed her lips and tears welled in her eyes. "He'll be so pissed off."

She spoke with the same tight-throated fear as the woman John encountered the week after the slumper killed Keith. It was a domestic violence call. She sat on a blood-stained couch crying, not because her bashed head was bleeding, but because she wouldn't tell John where her husband had gone. She kept saying he'd done nothing wrong. *It's my fault*, she said in that defeated voice. The next moment his partner shouted from the kitchen, *Suspect fleeing out the back door!* John burst out the front door, reaching the man as he scrambled into his car. It was blue like the sky, like Bijou's eyes. The door slammed shut. Lightening shot through his fingers and up his arm. He screamed. In seconds, John dangled from the car door by the fingers on his left hand as the pavement sped beneath him, kicking at his dragging heels, ripping the shoes from his feet. Two blocks away, the car took out the front window of the Seven-Eleven. In a blast of shattering glass and crunching metal, it came to a halt. John struggled to his feet. He couldn't free his fingers pinned inside the door. The man reached for the glove box and came back staring at John with desperate, fiery eyes. The man's lips moved like two slabs of wet clay and said, *Don't fuck with me, you bastard.* John felt for his pistol. The man swung a gun into John's face and John beat him to the draw. The world he knew exploded.

* * *

As John drove Bijou back to her cabin, she removed her gloves and held her hands over the heating vents in the dash. Her long fingers, barren of any rings, ended in short, trimmed nails.

"I bet you play guitar," John said, trying to lighten her mood.

"Yeah. Good guess." She sniffled and rubbed her hands together. Her voice brightened. "I'm playing at the Voyageur Saturday night. You should come."

"I don't make it to the bar too often." It would take an exceptional circumstance for John to go to the bar nowadays, too many *what ifs.* Bijou looked at him as if waiting for an explanation. "The crowds, noise, testosterone. Perfume. Makes me a little jumpy—unless I've had something to drink."

"Well, isn't that the idea of going to the bar?" She said. "To have a drink? Relax?"

He swallowed. Yes, drinking was what most people did, but that had been a problem back in the city—and a habit he worked hard to leave behind there. He didn't need AA. When he moved to Greenstone, he'd gone cold turkey and steered clear of the bar scene. He cleared his throat and looked back at her hands.

"You said Dan's your husband?"

"It's the ring thing, isn't it? Yeah. Got married when I was 19, been married five years—five years too long. I only wear my wedding ring when I'm not in the mood for men to hit on me." A laugh slipped from her lips.

He couldn't remember seeing any evidence of children back at the cabin.

"The only kids we got," she said as if reading his mind, "are those two goats. Danny got them for me from a breeder over on Portage Lake the first year we got married. Hans and Gretel. You like those names?"

He didn't have an opinion either way, but the way she said their names, as if they really were her children, he couldn't think of any other response but, "Yes."

She stared out the side window until the cabin came into view.

"You married?" Bijou said.

"Nope."

"Ever been?"

"Nope."

"Almost?"

"Once."

He fell in love with Audrey when she joined the department.

"Wish I could say almost," Bijou said, looking out the window.

Once he and Audrey got engaged, they moved in together. To make their private lives more bearable, they agreed not to ask about work at the dinner table. Home would be their refuge from the daily stresses of urban law enforcement. Whether they wanted to keep their agreement or not, it didn't really matter. Within a month, the slumper killed Keith and John was put on mandatory leave with counseling.

"Do you miss her?"

No one had ever asked. Her question took him by surprise almost as much as his answer.

"All the time."

As John withdrew into his depression, dinnertime with Audrey became as lifeless as the basement morgue. Eventually, he wouldn't talk about anything and instead of coming home, he went to the bar. Then the offer came through to come to Greenstone, and that was the end of that.

*   *   *

John made a follow up call to Bijou the next day.

"Just checking back with you on that trap line, and to be sure you're OK."

"I'm OK," she said.

"After yesterday I was a little concerned."

"Thanks, but I'm all right. Really."

Bijou sounded like a stranger, not the woman who helped him free the wolf or asked if he missed his ex-fiancé.

"I know why Dan was lying about that trap line." John's digging had unearthed a few revelations. According to property records and satellite images, the trapline was outside the Knutson's property. "That wolf in the snare? It was on reservation land. Did you know that?"

She didn't answer.

"I'm guessing that kind of violation might land a hefty fine, at least 50 foxes worth, especially for a guy who's not a band member. I really can't say though, because that would be up to the reservation game warden."

She was still silent.

"Could be worse. It's on record that last year Dan had his hunting privileges revoked for trespassing with intent to trap."

"So what are you saying?" Bijou finally said.

"As part of my daily filing, I need to make a referral report to the reservation game warden."

"What?"

"Is there anything you want me to add that I don't already know?" John said. "They'll handle it from there."

"Handle what?"

"Possible tres—"

"You don't have anything on Dan. Don't do this. Please."

"Bijou, I still have to make a report on what happened and what I do know."

"I'm sorry," she said. "I—if—It's just that Dan is not going to like this."

"Can you at least just do me one favor?" John said. The record also showed that Dan Knutson had been convicted of aggravated assault in Duluth a dozen years ago. Something about owing another man after the bar closed and paying him with a tire iron to the head. "From one neighbor to another, call me if there's anything I can do to help. Will you do that? Bijou?"

"OK," She said. Her voice relaxed. "Thanks. Really. I know you're just doing your job, but—you've been really decent to me."

* * *

Bijou called him the next day.

"Have you filed that report yet?" she asked.

"Not yet."

"I haven't told Dan that you know about that wolf being on reservation land." She sighed. "If you file that report, shit's gonna hit the fan."

"I have a job to do."

"I know. I'm just saying." Her voice strained. "You gotta tell me when you file that report. I don't want to be around when he hears about it."

"I understand."

"I hoped you would."

And so their conversations progressed with daily phone calls. It was crazy. He had more than 20 years on her, not to mention that he'd never mixed official business with personal before. In all his years of service not once did he cross that line until now. When she asked again about Audrey, he answered. He told her how he met Audrey and had to wait for years until she transferred to a different department before he could ask her out. That was as far as he got. John was a much better listener than he was a talker, so by the end of the week, he'd learned that Bijou was pregnant when she married Dan. Hans and Gretel were the names she'd chosen for the twins before she miscarried. And no matter how many times they tried again, they were no good at making babies.

"It did something to him," she said. "Something so secret and sad, he pushed it all deep inside and...well, sometimes..." Her voice trailed off. Silence filled the phone line until she whispered, "He scares me."

*   *   *

John decided Saturday night that he'd had his fill of work and nights alone. Enough chasing after intoxicated snowmobilers. Enough handing out citations to ice fisherman who hid coolers packed with northerns and crappies in their car trunks. Enough shooting wounded deer and moose with the 12-gauge before scraping their carcasses off the highway pavement. Instead, he found himself scrutinizing his appearance in the mirror—something he hadn't done since he had hair on the top of his head to scrutinize.

First, he went to his computer, and, though he'd been on the fence about it all week, he went ahead and emailed the trespassing report to the reservation game warden. Then he showered, shaved and put on fresh clothes. Wearing his knit cap and a camouflage jacket, he left for town as a civilian.

When John stepped through the back door of the Voyageur, he could hear Bijou. This time, chords from a guitar wrapped around her warbling voice as it cut through the din of activity.

"Howdy, stranger," Gloria, the bartender said.

A huge wooden canoe floated on an invisible river above their heads, suspended from the ceiling as if the whole bar were underwater. Two hooped beaver pelts framed the mirror behind the bar. Gloria smiled at him with recognition, brightening her faded face, worn by a two-pack-a-day habit and a lifetime of raising five kids. He knew Gloria more recently from trouble she was having with someone shooting deer on her land—turned out to be one of her sons from guess where? The Cities. No charges, but she was mad as hell.

"What can I get you?"

"A Bud Light."

He hardly recognized Bijou. Instead of the brown anorak and boots she'd worn when they released the wolf, Bijou had dipped herself in a long sapphire-blue sweater with matching tights capped off by black ankle boots. Her loose hair flowed back and forth like a mermaid's underwater. She sang with her eyes closed, her lips nearly kissing the microphone.

Gloria wrapped her hand around a sawed-off canoe paddle, pulled and filled his glass. The tap pulls were fashioned from various-shaped paddle handles, some glossy polyurethaned wood, others red or yellow plastic and aluminum. She handed John his beer.

"She's pretty good, you think?" she said, looking at Bijou.

He nodded, keeping his eyes on Bijou and handed Gloria a five dollar bill.

"That's it? You don't want to put it on a tab?"

"This is it."

"I can see you think she's a looker, too."

"You're not bad yourself, Gloria." He winked.

Gloria punched him on the shoulder. "Who'd have known you'd be the flirting kind. Better put your eyes back in your head, though, because she's taken. That's her husband there. You know Danny Knutson?"

John followed Gloria's thumb pointing down the bar at three men lined up on stools facing the flat screen television.

"He's the one on the end with the Vikings cap."

Dan, a stocky man in his mid-thirties, sat hunched over with his back to the stage watching football highlights. A blonde stood beside him wearing a black tank top and ropes of silver jewelry. She whispered in his ear.

"He's nice enough," said Gloria. "But a little rough around the edges."

"Well," John nodded and raised his glass to Gloria. "Cheers to pretty ladies." He hadn't taken a sip of alcohol and already he was in a good mood. He found a small table in the far back corner and stood to assess his surroundings. The pinball machine pinged and a foursome of men played pool under a deer-antler chandelier in the back room. About two dozen people sat at knotty pine tables facing the makeshift stage tapping their toes. A blast of cold air swept the floor every time a person passed through the front door.

Bijou caught his eye. She smiled and gave him a finger wave between guitar chords. He nodded back. The air grew stifling hot and sweat bloomed between his shoulder blades. He peeled off his jacket and sat with his back against the wall. He let out a long, slow sigh and took his first swig of beer in ten years. It tasted better than he ever remembered.

"Pool?" a friend asked.

"Sure. Why not?"

John's cue stick slid through his fingers like a well-oiled machine and his opponents' jaws dropped when he pocketed seven balls in a row. And the eight ball. At the end of two more games, he was three beers richer in wagers. Like cracked soil after a long drought, the beers quenched his thirst, swallow after swallow, until he finally relaxed and reclaimed his spot in the corner where the buzz of the bar had turned to a soothing hum.

Bijou abandoned her guitar on the stage and made the rounds. John watched as she fluttered among tables like a blue butterfly from flower to flower, staying just long enough to sip its nectar before searching for more. She stopped at the bar where Dan swatted her on the bottom. John's eyes narrowed. Her shoulders flinched, and she shrank away, her hands rubbing her arms as she hugged herself. The woman in the black tank top ignored Bijou and leaned over, saying something in Dan's ear. She pointed at John. Dan swiveled his head and locked eyes on him.

Dan spoke a few words to Bijou and turned back to face the television. Bijou wove her way through the now assembled crowd toward John.

"Hi," she said, the skip in her step now quashed, as if Dan had clipped her wings. A cheer rose from the men crowded around the television screen. "Thanks for coming," She raised her voice over the noise.

"You sound great," John said.

"I hope you're not leaving too soon. The band finally showed up." Off stage a woman warmed up with her guitar and another carried cymbals to the platform. "I've got to go help, but stay. Please?"

Why she thought he needed convincing to stay, he didn't know, because he would have stayed until the sun rose just to watch her. She gave his hand a quick squeeze as she left, sending a fire bolt to his belly. A bare-handed squeeze with no wedding ring.

Dan came over during a commercial break. On his feet, he was shorter than John expected. Above the belt, with a long, broad torso, he looked the part of a woodsman-for-hire. Below the belt, was another story. A stumpy pair of legs supported his mass and produced a comical duck waddle when he walked. Or, it might have been comical, if Dan hadn't taken himself so seriously. Once he got to John's table, he stood erect and uncomfortably close.

"Bijou says you're the C.O. who released that wolf."

John put out his hand. "John Reid."

"Daniel Knutson. I spoke to you on the phone." Dan's bear-like paw grasped John's hand. They gave each other a quick, strong hand shake. Dan's bloodshot eyes set slightly unfocused on John. "Bijou was real excited about that wolf. She couldn't stop talking about how it just about licked your packsacker ass in appreciation—I'm surprised Bijou didn't—or did she?" He laughed like a moose in rut, heavy and deep. His bravado couldn't camouflage the distrust in his voice. "She's like that. She can get dramatic. Exaggerate. She'll say things, do things she don't really mean."

"I was glad to help," John said. His fists clenched as his stomach tightened.

"I did just what you said. I put up new signs." Dan stuck his chin out and spoke slowly. "Shouldn't have no more trouble with that trespasser."

The sportscaster came back on the TV and caught Dan's attention. He gave John a silent nod, one last look—more like a glare—and waddled back to his stool without a second glance.

John gathered his jacket. Better to avoid confrontation before it began. Violence prevention 101. But just as he was going to call it quits for the night, Bijou started strumming her guitar again. She found him and made big ogle eyes at him, as if she'd read Dan's lips a moment ago. She shrugged one shoulder, smiled and sang a solo. It was the same song in the pole barn and it sent shivers to his toes. *And I am wanting...and I am needing you here...inside the absence of fear...* Just then, a draft swept across his feet. Dan was gone and so was the woman in the black tank top.

An hour, a beer and three whiskey shots later, John heard Bijou sing her last song. Only a scattering of diehards remained. A cymbal crashed off the stage and startled John into reaching for the pistol at his hip. Feeling its absence, he sat up straight and scanned the room like a startled watch dog. Gloria wiped down the bar and stacked glasses on the back side. The pool table was vacant. The television screens silent and black. As he stood to put on his jacket, he tripped on the table leg. He caught himself, but not before his beer glass tipped over and the dregs bled over the table top and onto the floor.

Bijou hauled a speaker off the platform.

"Can I give you a hand?" he asked.

"Sure." She passed the speaker to him. "Follow me." She grabbed another speaker and led him past the pool table to a closet where they stacked them on top of one another. "I am so happy you came tonight. And it's so sweet of you to stay and help. It's like you're my roadie." She winked and laughed.

"Anything for a rock star," he replied. It was the stupidest thing to say, but he was past caring.

"Did you see where Danny went?" she asked.

"He and his friends left a long time ago."

"Friends?" She raised an eyebrow. "You mean that woman he was with?"

His silence was answer enough.

Her soft smooth face turned hard. "Goddammit," she said under her breath. "How does he expect me to get home now?"

"I can give you a ride."

She looked at him with those blue eyes and smiled.

*   *   *

Outside, John opened the truck door for Bijou.
"Why thank you. Such a gentleman."

"My pleasure, Miss." Another dumb thing to say, but it made her laugh and he liked the sound of it.

"I don't think anybody has ever opened a door for me in my life—certainly not Danny."

"Dammit," John cried as he scraped his head climbing into the cab.

"Oh, that sounded like it hurt," she said. "Are you OK? Let me see."

He felt her cool hands on his head, pulling it down toward her. She pushed his hat up off his forehead. "Ouch," she said. "It's bleeding. Bad."

She pulled the first aid box from its mount beside the back seat and ripped open a package of gauze. "Hold still."

He couldn't take his eyes off her as she held his chin and wiped the wound clean.

"I think I love you," he said.

She looked at him, studied his face and stopped dabbing.

"You're drunk." She applied salve, a gauze pad and taped it over. "You are not driving."

Where was his training for what to do when he got drunk and had the most attractive wife of a felon drive him home? Shit, Officer Reid. This is a serious violation, goddammit, to allow someone—other than the officer—to drive the state's truck with access to his firearms.

*   *   *

"I think..." John said from the passenger seat as they drove past his house. "Yup, that was my place."

Bijou backed the truck up and pulled into the drive.

"It's right around the corner here, on the lake."

She drove in and stopped in front of the garage.

The skies had cleared and a half moon illuminated the surrounding snow. It turned the lake into a glimmering white plain. John climbed down from the passenger side and deliberately walked around the truck, extra careful not to slip on the ice. He tapped on the driver's window. Bijou lowered it a few inches.

"Turn the engine off," he said.

"I have to go home," Bijou said. "I'll bring the truck back in the morning."

"No," John said. "If you get caught with this or hit a deer or go in a ditch, I'm toast."

"If I don't go home soon..." She rolled the window down all the way. Her scent, a combination of sweat and perfume wafted out. "Hey, I really like you, and I'd like to stay, but..."

"Then stay," He said. He put his hand through the window. "Give me the keys."

She turned off the ignition and as she set the keys to the truck in his hand, he wrapped his fingers around hers.

*   *   *

Bijou sang. She sang and sang and sang.

John rolled over and reached for her warm softness beside him in the bed. She sang again. The sheets felt cold. He opened his eyes. It was the phone ringing, not Bijou's voice crooning in the darkness as she'd done last night, when the moon shone through the window, bathing the landscape of her body milky white. He picked up the phone.

"Hello?"

"John? Ed here." The sheriff.

John sat up straight. His head immediately announced a hangover with pounding pressure.

"You missing your truck?" He sounded wary and irritated.

John looked at his dresser. No keys. He couldn't see the truck in the driveway where Bijou had left it last night. Bijou—where was she?

"I've got a half-ton black Silverado super cab with plates that match yours. You're lucky, John. Your computer don't look like it's been touched, but there is some funny business going on—and you're going to need a new set of tires."

"Where are you?"

"County Road 27, in front of the Knutson's place."

*   *   *

The sheriff picked John up and drove him to the scene a few yards from the end of Dan and Bijou's driveway. John hopped out and circled the truck. A very large and very sharp blade had slashed all four tires flat.

"Looks like an axe done it," said the Sheriff. "I didn't notice at first, but when you check to see if anything's missing, looks like somebody left you a present." The sheriff paused a moment. A concerned tone laced his words. "Is everything all right with you, John? You're not in some kind of trouble you want to tell me about?"

John went to the driver's side window. Shit. The rifle was missing from the rack. The first aid box lay open on the floor and several pieces of bloody gauze lay scattered on the seat. When he felt for the gash on his forehead under his cap, it stung a nerve like a hot wire. He opened the door and something hit him in the face.

A snare hung from the top of the cab, its noose open wide and placed just so, at the perfect height for his head to slip through. John stepped back.

"Pretty weird, huh?" the sheriff said. "I'd say even creepy."

"Keys?"

"Didn't see any. I called Tony's and a tow should be here soon."

The sheriff's radio crackled, beckoning him back to his car. He returned and said, "John, you got yourself one hell of a mess here."

"I can see that, Ed."

"We're talking serious consequences."

John put his hands on his hips, set his lips and looked over and past Ed's shoulder.

"I'm trusting you on this," the sheriff continued. "And only because that was the dispatcher. I've got a crash with possible multiple fatalities over on 121. A goddam minivan full of teenagers took a turn too fast and rolled."

"Ed," John said looking the Sheriff straight in the eye. "This doesn't need to show up in the paper any time soon."

"I'll do my best." He clapped John on the shoulder. "But I can't make any promises."

The Sheriff's car roared up the highway and out of sight.

John's instinct told him not to touch anything. If he were in Minneapolis with a typical stolen vehicle, the county crime lab would have already shown up, dusting for prints, photographing and collecting evidence. But this was not Minneapolis. This was not a typical stolen vehicle.

John gathered the bloodied gauze and stuffed it into his jacket pocket. He returned the first aid box to its mount behind the seat. He was so thirsty, but the water bottle he kept in the door pocket was frozen rock solid. His head pounded and he felt sick to his stomach. The windows fogged up in no time and he began to shiver when his cell phone buzzed.

A text message from Bijou's phone.

DON'T FUCK WITH ME YOU BASTARD

John rubbed the stumps of his missing fingers. He stared out the clouded windshield. That's what the man back in Minneapolis had said before John killed him.

No sooner had the picture of the man's desperate face formed in John's mind than a shot rang out. John jerked his head toward the Knutson place. His stomach lurched and his tongue burned with bitterness. Another shot rang. He groped under the seat until his hand landed on the shotgun case. He pulled it out, assembled the gun, slid a shell into the chamber and seven more into the magazine.

"K540 Greenstone. K540," he said into the radio. "I am at 5420 CR 27 with a violent domestic. Suspect is Knutson, Daniel Allen DOB 1980, 00, 00. White male, brown hair, 5 foot 7, 180. He is armed with a .223 semi-automatic rifle and possible other weapons. He is with a possible female victim, status unknown. Request additional units and medics."

He dropped out of the truck, pulled the ballistic vest out from behind the seat and put it on. With the shotgun under his arm, he trotted to the gate, pausing at a no-trespassing sign nailed to the corner fence post. He shook his head. The red and white plastic was fresh and clean but with no signature. A third shot rang from the opposite end of the gravel lane. He rubbed his left fist, pumped the shotgun and strode up the drive into the purple shadows of the forest.

THE ACCIDENTAL BEEKEEPER
ALYSIA SAWCHYN

Four months after my twenty-third birthday, on a whim propped up by responsible finances, I moved to a small town in Indiana. There was something in the
interminable flatness and rows of corn that suggested the possibility of a pastoral
life. I lived in a small house on an acre of land on the east edge of town, a mile off
the bypass, three doors down from train tracks. The first time I saw the house,
in late spring, I drove in through the monotonous countryside, the clear sky an
overwhelming expanse pressing down the horizon, and wondered what I'd done.
But in the summer, my belief in the potential for contentment returned; wild corn
and roses grew unattended in the yard, and the local farmers' market was full of
cheap tomatoes and gallons of local honey. I lived with a man who worked long
hours and didn't mind that I wanted a yellow kitchen.

He said I made the house into a home. When I moved in, the living room
was littered with person-sized boxes and their squeaky styrofoam insides, even
though the man had already owned and lived in the house for two years. For him,
long hours meant working sunup to sundown two hours away. The house served
as a climate-controlled storage unit for his belongings and sometimes for his un-
conscious body. It was a quiet place. On weekends, he would stay in the town
where he worked, spend his nights haphazardly on couches or temporarily empty
beds. I spent the first two weeks putting things away, throwing light, unwieldy
boxes up through the small opening that led to the unfinished attic, vacuuming
ceiling fans, wiping down baseboards with a damp sponge. It was an ambitious,
industrious time. Once I ran out of things to arrange and dust, I turned my attention to the kitchen.

I'm not sure where my longstanding desire for a yellow kitchen came from,
but I'd built it up enough that it had the profundity of *something I'd always wanted*. After a lifetime of rented houses and apartments, I could and would choose
the color of a room, and this kitchen—too large, with a long window over the sink
where I kept empty glass bottles that caught the late morning light—was perfect,
the act of painting it a sign of permanence and stability in my life. I'd seen home
improvement commercials and believed painting a room was an effortless task,
an activity to finish in an afternoon, smiling.

The kitchen was supposed to be my project, but the man realized I'm awkward with a roller, unable to push hard enough into the wall. I spent hours pulling
up foot-wide sections of paint instead of putting them down, spent not enough

time waiting for the coats to dry. He came home and found me on the couch, hands over face, paint between fingers and under cuticles, a cigarette burning too close to my hair, a mug of tea in front of me. My head hurt from inhaling paint fumes, the soft spots in my skull buzzed.

He took over without asking, and I was relieved and resentful. The yellow I picked out was too pale by itself, he said, too much like a baby's room, so we went to the store his next day off and got a darker shade to paint the two opposing walls. Accent walls, he called them. He bought a better set of paint rollers and tasked me with scraping up lumps where the original fifteen-year-old coats of white paint had been layered on too thickly. If I dug in the putty knife at the right angle, it was like peeling down the loose skin near the base of my fingernails. I picked assiduously, compulsively, like I would until my fingers bled, until I found grey fuzz lining the walls. I stopped breathing and pointed.

"It's fine," he said. "We'll paint over it."

I couldn't pick at the walls anymore, so I sat outside on the back steps smoking, watching carpenter bees nestle deep into wooden support beams. But in the end, I had a yellow kitchen: two walls the color of a ripening avocado, two walls the color of farmer's honey.

*   *   *

The kitchen was my room. I learned how to make pumpkin rolls, chili, cornbread, mashed potatoes, anything in a crock pot, reaching out to my open-faced, earnest coworkers for their family recipes, straying from my prior costal diet of steamed vegetables and fish that the man found suspicious and unsubstantial. For our one year anniversary, the man bought me an old bicycle and bolted a mesh basket to its front, and I finally taught myself to ride. Weekly, I precariously balanced bags of produce and golden hued eggs from the farmers' market and cycled home over pothole-ridden roads. I had a routine, busied myself through the seasons. On Thursdays, I'd spend hours cooking enough food for the man to take away with him during the weekends and then entire years doing dishes, wanting the sink and countertops uncluttered so the refracting light from the glass bottles would bounce off the stainless steel unobstructed. Late Saturday mornings, I would stand quietly in the kitchen like a bird, one foot resting on top of the other, warming my hands around a mug of tea with too much honey.

One afternoon, in a patch of sun, the tip of a knife skidded off an avocado's slick pit, embedding itself in my right palm. I held my heartbeat in my hand, hot stinging came in measured beats. It was a weekday, and he was at his friend's, playing cards. I called him.

"I need you to come home," I said.

"Why?" he asked.

I looked and saw blood on the floor, blood on the knife, blood on the fruit.

"I can't tell how bad it is," I answered.

I cleaned the kitchen with my right arm uselessly bent, palm upturned and fingers pressed together to prevent drips, struggling to tear paper towels off the roll one handed. When he finally came home, I was lying on the couch exhausted, my hand weakly curled around a bandaid. He walked into the clean kitchen and came back out holding a near empty gallon of milk, frowning.

"You okay?" he asked.

"I think so."

"We're almost out of milk."

He shook the bottle to reinforce his point. I closed my eyes and rolled toward the inside of the couch, realizing that puncture wounds are unimpressive after the fact. I could feel him looking at me for a few moments before walking away to take a shower. He yelled from the bathroom, an afterthought, voice muffled by his shirt coming up over his face as he undressed, that the water I'd put on the stove was boiling over. I didn't move for a long time, listening to the water roiling and sputtering in the pot and onto the hot glass stovetop, and stood up only when he turned off the shower. Barely a half-inch of scalded water remained. I went to bed without making tea, left the jar of honey and mug with the dry teabag out on the counter in protest. Carpenter bees hibernate in the winter, sleep through hostile winds and cold. The following day, I got up and baked five batches of holiday cookies. Some I mailed off as thank you gifts; some he ate and took to friends' houses.

My palm healed slowly. For a few weeks after, I made poorly received stigmata jokes, even though I was told crucifixion nails were most likely put through the wrists, even though I knew better. There is still a scar, raised but camouflaged by the lines in my palm. A mild sense of martyrdom is appealing because of the virtue attached to the suffering; saints are remembered and venerated for their sacrifices. The stability and permanence embodied by my yellow kitchen, my routines, felt more like drudgery than solace and became weights I carried, showily, through that winter to the next.

If you ask him, he'll say he left me, that it was his decision. That's only half true, though. Really, he couldn't wait for me to make up my mind about whether or not I wanted to stay.

*   *   *

A pastoral life. I now live with a woman whose mother keeps bees. She comes back from family visits with jars and jars of honey and an illicitly-obtained epi pen. I ask if she is allergic.

"Bees are funny," she answers.

She is lying on the kitchen table, feet planted on the seat of a wicker chair. She tells me the more often a person is stung by a honeybee, the more likely she is to experience anaphylactic shock. She picks at her cuticles with a nail clipper while explaining. I make an interested, assenting noise while piling dishes into the sink.

She considers her fingers, tells me it doesn't matter how I remove a honeybee's stinger, just that I do it as quickly as possible.

"I haven't heard from him in a while," I reply. "Thankfully."

She nods.

There are too many animals in our small, rented apartment, and cats twine around my legs, paw open the kitchen cabinets while my hands are too busy to shoo them away. The dog, chewing on a plastic bottle he stole from the recycling pile, commandeers the sunlit patch of carpet in front of the balcony door. Our lease is expiring soon, and neither of us knows where we are going, only that it will be far away from where we are now.

The only yellow on the kitchen walls is spattered grease. I keep honey in a cabinet above the stove and stash ripening avocados in a dish by the cluttered sink. I know the water in the kettle is almost ready when the bees inside it flap their wings so hard they make a tinny, buzzing sound. I am happy.

FIGHTING SEASONS
RANDY BROWN

Even a city boy from Eastern Iowa
follows the markets, like sports, on the A.M. radio
and has a vague sense of the harvests to come.

Feeder calves and pork-belly futures, forecasts for soybeans and corn
fill our diner conversations and our mouths
like bushel-bags of baseball stats, ideals and speculations.

The Cubs might finally do it this fall. And El Niño could make a comeback.
Into this familiar world, armed with coffee and pie,
a waitress gently probes toward our war: *Heard anything from your sons?*

Floods and droughts, blizzards and winds
are no strangers to the plains. We work the land,
the land works us. We do our jobs. Weather either happens, or it doesn't.

It is winter in Eastern Afghanistan, but spring is coming.
There are no crops of poppies there—that's down south.
News is, the fighting will soon resume. At least, that's what the papers say.

Maybe this year will finally be our year.

CONTRIBUTORS

James Barnett is a former journalist, commodities trader, and teacher. His fiction has been published in *Thrasher* magazine, and his poetry has been published in *American Goat*. He now spends most of his time raising his two young sons.

Scott Beal's first book of poems, *Wait 'Til You Have Real Problems*, was published by Dzanc Books in November 2014. His poems have recently appeared in *Rattle, Prairie Schooner, Beloit Poetry Journal, Southern Indiana Review, Sonora Review,* and other journals. He won a 2014 Pushcart Prize. He serves as writer-in-the-schools for Dzanc Books in Ann Arbor and teaches in the Sweetland Center for Writing at the University of Michigan.

Randy Brown was preparing for deployment to Eastern Afghanistan in 2010 as a member of the Iowa Army National Guard's 2nd Brigade Combat Team, 34th Infantry "Red Bull" Division. After a paperwork snafu dropped him from the deployment list, he retired with 20 years of military service and a previous overseas deployment. He then went to Afghanistan anyway, embedding with Iowa's Red Bull units as a civilian journalist from May-June 2011. A freelance writer in central Iowa, Brown blogs about military topics at: www.redbullrising.com. His non-fiction and poetry have appeared in *So It Goes: The Literary Journal of the Kurt Vonnegut Memorial Library; The Journal of Military Experience; Line of Advance; O-Dark-Thirty;* and *The Pass In Review,* as well as the first three volumes of the anthology series, *Proud to Be: Writing by American Warriors*, published annually by the Southeast Missouri State University Press.

Lisa J. Cihlar's poems have appeared in *Blackbird, South Dakota Review, Green Mountains Review, Crab Creek Review,* and *Southern Humanities Review*. She was twice nominated for Pushcart Prizes and two Best of the Net nominations. She has authored three chapbooks: *The Insomniac's House* (Dancing Girl Press), *This is How She Fails* (Crisis Chronicles Press) and *When I Pick Up My Wings from the Dry Cleaner,* a chapbook contest winner at Blue Light Press. She lives in rural southern Wisconsin.

Lee Colin Thomas lives and writes in Minneapolis, Minnesota. He received a Loft Mentor Series Award in poetry (selected by Kristin Naca and E. Ethelbert Miller) and an honorable mention for the Minnesota Emerging Writers Grant. Lee's poems have appeared in *Poet Lore, Salamander, The Gay and Lesbian Review Worldwide, Water~Stone Review,* and elsewhere.

Sara Crow is an award-winning short story writer who found characters in the strangest places since she told her mother her imaginary friend's backstory at three years old. She continues to hope to enchant her readers (which include, most commonly, her husband and four cats) from her home in the middle of Kansas.

Gary Dop—poet, scriptwriter, essayist, and actor—lives with his wife and three daughters in the foothills of the Blue Ridge Mountains, where he is an English professor at Randolph College. Dop's first book of poems, *FATHER, CHILD, WATER*, is forthcoming from Red Hen Press in 2015. Dop was awarded the Great Plains Emerging Writer Prize, a Special Mention in the Pushcart Prize Anthology, and his essays have aired on public radio's *All Things Considered*. His poems have appeared in *Prairie Schooner, North American Review, Agni, New Letters, Poetry Northwest*, and *Rattle*, among others.

Ryan Dzelzkalns is a midwestern boy at heart. He moved to the big city to pursue his dreams and an MFA from New York University.

Chris Haven was born in Oklahoma, back when people thought that was part of the Midwest. His poetry has appeared or is forthcoming in *Whiskey Island, the museum of americana, Waccamaw*, and *Poet Lore*. He teaches creative writing at Grand Valley State University in Michigan and has recently finished a novel.

Henry Heidger is a writer and poet. He lives in St. Louis, Missouri.

Marianna Hofer has Studio 13 in the gloriously haunted Jones Building in Findlay, Ohio. Her poems and stories appear in small magazines, and her b&w photography hangs in local exhibitions and eateries. Her first book, *A Memento Sent by the World*, was published by Word Press in 2008.

Ben Hoffman is the author of a chapbook, *Together, Apart*. His fiction has won the *Chicago Tribune's* Nelson Algren Award and *Zoetrope: All-Story's* Short Fiction Contest and appears online at *American Short Fiction, Juked, Tin House,* and elsewhere. He is the 2014-2015 Carol Houck Smith Fellow at the Wisconsin Institute for Creative Writing.

Matt Hurley was born and raised in Upstate New York. He lived in Chicago for five years after college. His story, "One Swing," is inspired by the many nights and weekends he spent in Chicago parks pitching for middling men's league teams. He now resides in the Boston area where he works as a marketing writer and is retired from the game of softball.

Anna Lea Jancewicz lives in Norfolk, Virginia, where she homeschools her children and haunts the public libraries. She is an Associate Editor at *Night Train*, and her writing has appeared or is forthcoming at *Atticus Review, Hobart, matchbook, Prime Number, WhiskeyPaper*, and many other venues. Yes, you CAN say Jancewicz: Yahnt-SEV-ich. More at: http://annajancewicz.wordpress.com/

Jessie Janeshek's first book of poems is *Invisible Mink* (Iris Press, 2010). She is an Assistant Professor of English and the Director of Writing at Bethany College. She holds a Ph.D. from the University of Tennessee-Knoxville and an M.F.A. from Emerson College. She co-edited the literary anthology *Outscape: Writings on Fences and Frontiers* (KWG Press, 2008).

Elizabeth Kerper lives in Chicago and recently graduated from DePaul University with a BA in English literature. Her work has appeared in *Eclectica, NEAT,* and *N/A Literary Magazine,* where she is a contributing editor. She can generally be found sitting quietly in the corner with her nose stuck in a book.

Leonard Kress has published fiction and poetry in *Solstice, Passages North, Massachusetts Review, Iowa Review, American Poetry Review, Atticus Review, Harvard Review, The Writing Disorder, Barn Owl Review,* etc. His recent collections are *The Orpheus Complex, Living in the Candy Store,* and *Thirteens.* He teaches philosophy, religion, and creative writing at Owens College in Ohio.

Jillian Merrifield is a graduate of DePaul University's MA in Writing and Publishing program and currently teaches composition at the College of Lake County in Grayslake, Illinois. Her work has previously appeared in *Midwestern Gothic* and the *Curbside Splendor* E-zine.

Rachel Proctor May has written for publications including *McSweeney's Internet Tendency, Texas Observer, blue,* and *Canvas.* She is a former staff writer for the *Austin Chronicle.* Her favorite month is November.

Lisa Mecham's work has appeared in *Juked, Carve,* and *Barrelhouse Online,* among other publications. Lisa has served as a reader for *Tin House* and as an editor for *Origins Literary Journal.* A midwesterner at heart, she lives in Los Angeles where she continues to write a little bit of everything. More at lisamecham.com.

Todd Mercer won the first Woodstock Writers Festival's Flash Fiction contest. His chapbook, *Box of Echoes,* won the Michigan Writers Cooperative Press contest and his digital chapbook, *Life-wish Maintenance,* is forthcoming from RHP Books. He's a multi-year judge of the Amazon Breakthrough Novel Awards and the Independent Publisher Poetry Awards for Poetry. Mercer's poetry and fiction appear in *Apocrypha & Abstractions, Blink Ink, Blue Collar Review, The Camel Saloon, Camroc Press Review, Cease, Cows, Cheap Pop, Dunes Review, East Coast Literary Review, Eunoia Review, Falling Star, 50-Word Stories, The Fib Review, Gravel, The Lake, The Legendary, Main Street Rag Anthologies, Melancholy Hyperbole, Misty Mountain Review, Mobius: The Journal of Social Change, theNewer York, One Sentence Poems, Postcard Poems and Prose, Postcard Shorts, Right Hand Pointing, River Lit, The Second Hump,* and *Spartan.*

Corey Mertes is an attorney, a former casino pit boss, and a ballroom dance instructor with a degree in economics from the University of Chicago and an MFA in film and television from the University of Southern California. His stories have appeared in *2 Bridges Review, Green Briar Review, Bull: Men's Fiction, Valparaiso Fiction Review, Poydras Review, The Prague Revue, Hawai'i Review*, and many other journals.

Linda Niehoff's short fiction has appeared or is forthcoming in *Necessary Fiction, Bartleby Snopes, Dogzplot, Boston Literary Magazine*, and others. She's lived in Kansas her whole life and is a fan of silver water towers, ghost stories, and instant cameras.

Nick Ostdick is a husband, runner, and writer who lives and works in Western Illinois. He holds an MFA in creative writing from Southern Illinois University and edited the hair-metal-inspired anthology, *Hair Lit, Vol. 1* (Orange Alert Press, 2013). He's the winner of the Viola Wendt Award for fiction and his stories have been nominated for a Pushcart Prize. His work has appeared in *Exit 7, Annalemma, Big Lucks Quarterly, The Emerson Review*, and elsewhere.

Charlotte Pence is the author of the soon to be released *Many Small Fires* (Black Lawrence Press, January 2015) and has previously published *The Branches, the Axe, the Missing* (Black River chapbook prize winner, 2012), and *Weaves a Clear Night* (Flying Trout Press Chapbook winner, 2011). A professor of English and creative writing at Eastern Illinois University, Pence also edited *The Poetics of American Song Lyrics* (University Press of Mississippi, 2012) that explores the similarities and differences between poetry and song. Her awards include the Discovered Voices prize, multiple Pushcart nominations, and the New Millennium Writing award. And her new poetry has recently been published in *Alaska Quarterly Review, Denver Quarterly, North American Review, Prairie Schooner*, and *The Southern Poetry Anthology*.

Rachel Richardson was born in Tulsa, Oklahoma, in 1987. She has lived in coastal Carolina, upstate New York, and Vienna, Austria. She currently lives in upstate South Carolina, and works at Hub City Press. Her work has appeared or is forthcoming from *Wyvern Lit, Gigantic Sequins, Revolution House, Passages North*, and elsewhere. "Dirt" is one of fifty short pieces, one per state, that comprise her book *State*. You can find her online at www.richardsonrachel.com or on Twitter @pintojamesbean.

Alysia Sawchyn is a graduate student and first-year composition instructor currently living in small-town Indiana. She often threatens to move to the West Coast and sell baked goods out of her car. She holds a BA in creative writing from the University of Tampa.

Wendy A. Skinner's stories have appeared in *The Potomac Journal of Politics and Poetry, Monkeybicycle, Dust & Fire*, and elsewhere. "Trespassing" is from a short story collection written with support from a 2014 Minnesota State Arts Board Artist Initiative Grant. Her book, *Life with Gifted Children: Infinity & Zebra Stripes*, won the Arizona Glyph Award, and she's the 2010 recipient of the Carol Bly Award in Non-Fiction. She holds an MFA from Hamline University and lives in Minneapolis. www.

wendyaskinner.com.

Sam Slaughter is a writer based in DeLand, Florida. He serves as the Book Review Editor for *The Atticus Review* and has had both fiction and nonfiction published in a variety of places, including *McSweeney's Internet Tendency, South85, Heavy Feather Review, and The Review Review*. He can be found online at his website, www.samslaughterthewriter.com, and on Twitter @slaughterwrites.

Lindsey Steffes is working on her MFA in Fiction at University of California Riverside. Currently, she is writing *American Candy*, a collection of short stories exploring the loneliness, mysticism, and magic inherent in the Midwest. As a storyteller and Wisconsin native, she focuses on characters with small-town ideals, eccentricities of spirit, and candid voices reflecting the reality of the world she grew up in.

Greg Walklin's writing has appeared in *The Millions, the Ploughshares Blog,* and *Necessary Fiction*. He regularly reviews books for the *Lincoln Journal-Star* and has fiction forthcoming in *Palooka Magazine*. An attorney, he and his wife, Tiffany, live in Lincoln, Nebraska.

Marcus Wicker is the author of *Maybe the Saddest Thing* (Harper Perennial), selected by DA Powell for the National Poetry Series. Wicker's awards include a 2011 Ruth Lilly Fellowship, Pushcart Prize, as well as fellowships from Cave Canem, and The Fine Arts Work Center. His work has appeared in *Poetry, American Poetry Review,Third Coast, Ninth Letter*, and many other magazines. Marcus is assistant professor of English at University of Southern Indiana and poetry editor of *Southern Indiana Review*. He serves as director of the New Harmony Writers Workshop.

Lauren Crawford is an Ann Arbor-based writer and editor with a penchant for telling jokes poorly and a passion for writing in the margins. Her first published poem was about a unicorn, and it was written exclusively in rhyming couplets (she was ten at the time). She loves science fiction novels, Suprematism, and survival horror video games, and has begun to run out of places to properly store her books. She still writes about unicorns. Find her at www.lauren-crawford.com.

Jessica Dewberry's work appears in the *Los Angeles Review of Books*, *Mutha Magazine*, and other places. She's an assistant nonfiction editor for *Pithead Chapel*, a literary journal based in Michigan. For decades, her relatives lived in the infamous Cabrini-Green projects in Chicago before most of the units were demolished. She also visited the city biannually, for a few years, and once experienced a winter storm that caused her to cease all complaints about winters she's experienced elsewhere, especially in southern California where she lives and works.

Cammie Finch loves tea and hula-hooping. She is a junior at the University of Michigan, studying Creative Writing and English. Her favorite ice cream is vanilla drizzled with maple syrup, and her favorite poets are Pablo Neruda and Sylvia Plath. Her favorite book is always the one she is currently reading. Three of her favorite words include betwixt, akimbo, and kerfuffle. After graduation, Cammie hopes to spend a summer writing a novel on a Dutch houseboat, attend an Indian wedding, and increase the world's love for audiobooks, one expressive voice at a time.

J. Joseph Kane is a poet and fiction writer from Michigan. His work has appeared in *The Newer York, Clapboard House, Elimae, RHINO, Cricket Online Review, Psychic Meatloaf, Right Hand Pointing, The Splinter Generation*, and others. He grew up on Lake Huron and loves the smell of water.

Mackenzie Meter is a born-and-raised Michigander with a love for running, hammocking, and homemade soups. She currently works as the marketing manager for an Ann Arbor brewery, where she gets to write about (and enjoy) excellent beer. A lifelong reader, writer, and lover of words, she couldn't be more thrilled to be a part of *Midwestern Gothic*.

Jamie Monville is a senior studying English the University of Michigan. She has been known to fall in love with beautiful sentences, flawed characters, and home decor. Jamie has a passion for hand lettering and creating handmade unlined journals. She is looking to pursue a career in publishing after she graduates.

Kelly Nhan is a senior studying English and Women's Studies at the University of Michigan, and originally from Connecticut. She loves finding good coffee places, exploring cities, reading good poetry, and chatting about feminism. She is interested in going into book publishing, or eventually going to grad school to study postcolonial literature and feminist theory.

Christina Olson is the author of a book of poems, *Before I Came Home Naked*. Her poetry and nonfiction recently appeared in *The Normal School, Gastronomica,* and *RHINO*. She lives in Georgia and online at www.thedrevlow-olsonshow.com.

C.J. Opperthauser writes in his kitchen and blogs at http://thicketsandthings.tumblr.com.

Jeff Pfaller is a novelist and short story writer. His short fiction has appeared or is forthcoming in *Jupiter, North Chicago Review,* and *Fiction on the Web*. A Midwesterner through and through since the day he was born, Jeff has transplanted his wife, two children, dog, and cat from Michigan to Des Plaines, Illinois.

Robert James Russell is the author of two upcoming books: the collection *Don't Ask Me to Spell It Out* (WhiskeyPaper Press, 2015) and the novel *Mesilla* (Dock Street Press, 2015). His first novel, *Sea of Trees,* was published in 2012. He was recently awarded a University Musical Society Residency for the 2014-2015 season. You can find him online at robertjamesrussell.com.

THE
LOS ANGELES
REVIEW

FICTION. POETRY. ESSAYS. REVIEWS.
SUBMIT. SUBSCRIBE.

REDHEN PRESS

DIVERGENT, WEST COAST
LITERATURE

18911164R10082

Made in the USA
Middletown, DE
28 March 2015